The Kelpie

– JOHN GOLDSWORTHY –

Seasons
Shel one of the
best! [illegible]

An environmentally friendly book printed and bound in England by
www.printondemand-worldwide.com

Mixed Sources
Product group from well-managed forests, and other controlled sources
www.fsc.org Cert no. TT-COC-002641
© 1996 Forest Stewardship Council
FSC

PEFC Certified
This product is from sustainably managed forests and controlled sources
www.pefc.org
PEFC
PEFC/16-33-415

This book is made entirely of chain-of-custody materials

FastPrint Publishing
www.fast-print.net/store.php

The Kelpie

All characters are fictional.
Any similarity to any actual person is purely coincidental.

ISBN 978-178035-377-7

First published 2012 by
FASTPRINT PUBLISHING
Peterborough, England.

Prologue

A dark shape emerged from the small cluster of trees standing almost on the edge of the sombre loch. Still now, as the night breeze softened to allow the leaves to hang limp and lifeless. Many had already fallen in the approach of autumn and branches were unprotected against the violent storms that beset the waters in the hard winter that was to come.

Circling in a perfect arc to alight on its favourite perch, the Long Eared Owl executed a well rehearsed landing and settled its feathers in a soft downward caress of its body. Then it too, was still and invisible to any onlooker.

Down below, scurrying back and forth were the myriad inhabitants of the small woody area of the coniferous forest. Small mammals and insects about their nightly hunt for food, themselves being both hunter and hunted. The motionless owl watched, uninterested as its digestive system continued to macerate the small mice and voles it had caught earlier.

An unknown presence entered its peripheral vision. From its vantage point, the owl had a vast knowledge of all and every regular movement from its years of operation in the territory. He swivelled his head in a smooth, well oiled fashion, like a war-time gun turret.

Down below the shapes that had disturbed him moulded into the forest floor, too dim to distinguish the outline of the intruder. Or were there two?

His ears could pick up no sound, his eyes no movement. But something was there that did not belong.

A sense of uneasiness and apprehension, alien to his kind, affected his composure. He was the hunter, nothing hunted him except humans, and he was aware of a feeling that his prey would have had as he swooped to kill.

He remained absolutely still and watched.

Although there was no sound from the shapes, a dialogue between them continued in a kind of mind transference. Each understood the other and speech was not necessary. That was the way it had always been since time began. Speech was only sounds contorted into words that portrayed the thoughts in humans. Their only means of direct communication. If minds were attuned properly then ideas, viewpoints, theories, conceptions were only a matter of appreciation by the other tuned in participant.

Then it has to be done, was the thought conveyed to the other.

We are agreed then.

It is what we have believed in since we became aware.

The time is tomorrow. We must prepare.

I am ready. The signs are in favour and I am content that we shall end our days as we would wish.

Good. There is much to do before daybreak.

The owl did not actually see the shapes disperse, nor see which way they went, only a feeling that he was alone with his regular companions again. His true ears below the sharp feathers masquerading as 'ears' picked up a soft swirl as the waters opened to admit visitors and immediately afterwards a sharp crack as if an otter had slapped the surface with a swipe of his tail.

The two shapes previously stood beneath the Scots pine slowly submerged into the dark depths of the loch, swimming strongly to reach the haven one hundred and thirty feet beneath the protecting water that had been their home for a time that man could not measure.

Chapter One

'The heavens could never hold this much bloody water,' swore the lone motorist, swerving to avoid a large puddle swirling inwards to the centre of the road. Water ran everywhere. Teeming down through the trees and thundering onto her bonnet and roof as if it were intent on beating the thin metal into a flat wreck. 'That's what it'll do if I don't get some protection soon,' she cursed again.

Tranches of heavy gusts swept over the grim tarmac, immediately to be driven horizontally into her windshield as the force four gale whipped up a maelstrom in the nearby loch.

'Why did I ever agree to come on this so called holiday?' Kate MacManus questioned her own judgement at attempting a trip so far north. Not only north, but across the border where she had sworn she would never go again.

'It will do you good after what you have been through,' her colleague Marjorie had said. 'You need to get away from it all.' How many times had Kate heard that phrase, trotted out as if it would solve all the world's problems.

I don't have a problem any more she thought. Once, yes. But now I've got over it and am starting a new life. I was all right until everybody said that I should take time off to recover.

How do you recover from a broken heart? With time, yes. With compassion from others, yes. With understanding and no meddling, yes. But despite her misgivings she had relented when her childhood friend, Annie had called to offer her a rent free holiday in the Scottish Highlands where she now lived.

Annie McBride! The scourge of the fifth form. Nothing was too outlandish for her. And she had proved it when she had run off with a sixteen year old lad to Gretna Green and moved to Scotland to take up a country life with her husband's family.

Kate had met with Annie many times since then. But only in fleeting trips to a half-way point for a day or two's reminiscences. She swore she would never attempt another trip to Scotland after her bitter experience some years previously when it had rained continuously during her so called week's "holiday of a lifetime" as the brochure had succinctly put it.

Now her worst fears were coming to fruition. It was raining like she had never seen it before. And what's more, she thought she heard the dreaded sound of thunder up ahead, as a precursor to more bad weather.

And she still had a further fifteen miles or so to go.

Kate checked, pulled over into the only dry piece of land she could find and peered at her map. According to Annie's instructions, the cottage was tucked deep into a rise overlooking the loch with a backdrop of one of Scotland's dour mountains sheltering the rear of the property. That didn't help when the route was almost blinded by the incessant rain and the road signs, what little there were, were unreadable or missing.

As this is the only road north and it started out as the right one, Kate checked her map for the road reference – yes the A835 – the one that followed the A9 from Edinburgh, oh how she wished that she had stayed there until the weather improved. But headstrong and undeterred by the cautious comments of her fellow companions in the Lion Hotel, she had persevered, wanting to get to Annie's place as quickly as possible.

That was out of the question now as the storm quickened, rocking the small Honda Civic with its power. Better lay off for a while, she thought. Can't drive anyway, as the wipers can't keep up with the water. For the past five miles or so, she had driven in a facsimile of an old black and white picture show where sight was limited to regular stabs of visions.

Thank god I brought a flask with me. Still hot she found out as she poured the precious coffee into the cup. And sweet. Nothing like a mountain of sugar to bring an ordinary coffee to life. And me as well.

Suddenly the roar of the rain and wind died and receded across the loch like a curtain being drawn backwards across a cornfield. A little light broke through the dark overcast sky and shimmered its image on the eerie rippled surface.

Her old Honda still blasted out the warmth on top control and Kate reached for the knob to ease the fan. As she leant over, she caught a glimpse of something down by the loch side. Her car was about a hundred yards from the edge from where the thickly gorsed ground sloped precariously down to where the water battled with the weeds.

Is that a man? she cried, almost screaming her protest at such a foolhardy stunt. For surely that was what it was, if anyone was out and about in this weather. She stopped to reprimand herself. Well you are aren't you? Too engrossed to continue her argument she watched through the storm created mist as the man moved slowly along the shore. Disappearing and emerging in irregular patterns, the man, if that was what it was, continued slowly towards the nearby woodland of firs and pines.

Whatever could anyone be doing at this time of night? And in this weather? Then she told herself that she had imagined the whole thing, just like those schooldays looking at clouds and telling each other what they saw. Some of the sightings were pure imagination, and some so obvious that it made some of them blush at the description. Especially by Annie! She always saw the crudest impressions first.

The persistent drizzle over the loch beat up the water again with a champagne fizz that caught the moon's light in a fairy dance across to the far side. Another shape came into view from the direction of the wood. This time more pronounced. It was a horse, wasn't it she asked herself? Yes. A horse. Again, what was a loose horse doing out of its stable on a night like this?

It moved slowly along the shore in the opposite direction to the one the man had taken. Was it his? Had he released it from somewhere? Kate watched, hardly daring to breathe without realising that at a hundred yards, no one could have heard her anyway.

Another swirl of the mist covered the image and when the expected movement did not re-emerge from the other side, Kate looked piercingly at where she estimated the thing to be. Only the deep ripple of waves outward in concentric circles met her gaze, as if someone or something had entered the moment before. Then the mist lifted and everywhere was empty.

Kate could not convince herself that she had seen something, but with the conditions as they were, perhaps she had been mistaken and her mind had made up a picture of what her eyes thought they saw. She thought of all the magician's tricks that so deceived the eyes, that you thought it was really magic, but in truth you knew it wasn't.

She finished her coffee and started her car, ready for the last lap to where she longed for a comfortable chair, a good glass of wine, or scotch? to relax her after hours and hours of concentrated driving.

She left the loch to its secrets.

Chapter Two

Her host, Annie McBride was overjoyed to see her and clasped her to her ample bosom in the warm embrace of very good friends.

'I thought you'd never get here in this weather,' she said as she helped Kate remove her coat and scarf. 'It's been hours since you left Edinburgh and I was beginning to worry.'

'It seemed like days to me,' laughed Kate, now fully accustomed to the fiery glow of the logs in the stone hearth and the almost reviving glow of the lights so missed in the darkness of the lonely journey. 'Thank god for my little Honda.'

'I've never known it so rough in all the time I've lived here.' Annie disappeared to the kitchen and returned with a bottle of malt whisky and two glasses. 'I don't suppose you'll say no to a little body warmer?'

'Too true I won't. I've pictured that all the way here. And a cosy place to hide all that dark and gloomy scenery that you call Scottish beauty.'

'Ha! Wait till you see it in its proper light, then you'll change your mind.' Annie finished her drink and cocked one eyebrow. 'Another?'

Kate held her glass out and watched the honey coloured liquid hit the bottom. 'I'll reserve my judgement on that.

The only other time that I had experienced in these parts some ten years ago in the seventies, it rained all the week. Swore I'd never come again.'

'But here you are and we are going to have a cracking time while you're here weather or no weather.' Annie's glass was now being warmed in the palms of her hands as she looked closely at her friend. 'You are OK aren't you? I mean ...'

'Yes, of course I'm OK. Apart from the hundreds of nosy people who keep telling me that it will pass and I will be back to normal again.' Kate studied the pine logs as they spat out sparks and crackled as if to refute her confidence.

'How long has it been now? Three, four months?'

'Nearly four months.' Kate paused. 'But I'm well and truly over it now, if you ever can get over it.' She shook her head. 'Let's not talk about it tonight. I'm tired and a little confused.'

'About what?'

'Oh, you know, the way I'm feeling right now, the doubts, and the fears and the lack of confidence.' Kate shrugged her shoulders and attempted to pass it off with a forced laugh which did nothing to allay the depressive mood she was in. 'Sorry if I'm not good company at the moment, but I have these doubts all the time and have even imagined things on my way here.'

'You are bound to have those sort of inner emotions from time to time. I know I did, and they lasted far longer than I thought they would.'

Kate started slightly. 'I'm sorry. I was so absorbed with my own problems that I'd completely forgotten yours. That's very selfish of me. Forgive me for being so insensitive.'

'Nothing to apologise for. Compared to your troubles, mine was miniscule.' Annie laughed in that unique fashion that had first attracted Kate to her at the High School some fifteen years ago.

'My bloke just buggered off without a by your leave or kiss my arse, if you'll pardon the expression.'

Kate remembered the outgoing girl, who outshone every other student in her initial years, only to drop off as she approached the final two years as a student. She was far too fond of boys and flirting and living it up for all she was worth. But despite her waywardness, there was a deep feeling of loyalty when it came to the friendship between them. Whereas Kate was ultra cautious and sometimes too withdrawn, Annie bragged about every escapade she had experienced. Some of them not for the ears of the teachers or her parents, who had given up on her, but mostly for her fellow classmates who hung on her every word.

Then finally to cap it all, she ran off with her current boyfriend to Gretna Green, married him and set up home in Scotland with his bakery business parents. It was a shock to the whole school, and especially Kate who had so valued her close relationship.

Annie wrote to Kate often, describing the "wonderful life" in Scotland and how she was hoping to get her own place away from the in-laws. Kate missed her terribly but wrote regularly, until the replies became spasmodic and finally stopped some four years ago. Her last letters had been returned "gone away."

'What happened?' Kate's question took Annie by surprise.

'He met someone else didn't he?' There was no remorse in her tone. Just a statement of fact.

'Did you suspect anything?'

'Nah. You don't do you?' Annie said defiantly. 'Last one to know.'

'I'm sorry it turned out like this,' said Kate and leant over to touch Annie's hand.

'I'm not. Not now. You were right you know. You warned me that we were too young. But people of that age don't listen do they?' She turned her face to the fire. 'We could have made a go of it, if we hadn't had to live with his family. They ruled his life and mine. We were just lodgers, working for them. That's not a marriage, and Andy knew it too.'

'So how did you end up here?' Kate looked around the neat little cottage at the pretty curtains and the corded carpet, easy and comfortable chairs with a dining table under the window at the rear. 'It's everything you imagine a country cottage to be. Your taste hasn't changed. I remember the designs you used to do in class of all sorts of subjects. Dresses, furniture, lampshades, even gardens. You were brilliant.'

'Not brilliant enough at sizing up a man though was I?' She poured another shot of the whisky and indicated to Kate that she should help herself. She declined.

'I don't blame Andy, funnily enough. He was constricted by the situation and couldn't wait to get out at night. I was too tired most of the time, working in the bakery, cooking when I came home – oh yes!' she interjected as Kate raised her head. 'I was the one who cleaned, cooked, and was a general dogsbody to the whole family.'

'Oh my god. I never realised it was as bad as that. You never said in your letters.'

'I was too proud wasn't I?' Annie's head jerked up as if to confirm the fact.

There was a silence between them. Finally Kate spoke. 'When you finally wrote and asked me to come to visit you, it was like as if the years had fallen away and we were back at school again. I forgot my depression. Your letter lifted me like no one had been able to do since … well since …. you know.'

'Why don't you say it Kate?' Annie's challenging eyes looked straight at Kate.

'Say what?'

'What I know you have been keeping in a closet in your head all these months. How do I know? Because it's what everyone does. They won't admit the facts. Facts that should be divorced from feelings so that they can be looked at objectively and not with any emotional baggage attached to them.'

'You'd have made a very good psychiatrist, you know,' said Kate, smiling despite her misgivings. 'And you're right of course. The word that I've avoided for so long is . . "dead."'

'And one other I think,' said Annie.

'Which one … ? I don't understand.'

'Murdering bastard!' Annie almost shouted the words.

Kate sat stunned. Unable to grasp the implication of what she knew was the truth.

Annie in turn rose and cradled her friend in her arms. 'Let it go Kate. You have cried for all the rest of your family and how they were affected, but you have never cried for yourself alone.' She kissed her forehead tenderly. 'Cry now. Let it all go. It needs to be released.'

Chapter Three

A lone walker strode purposely along the same route as Kate had taken just a week before. His gait was steady and smooth. Each foot placed precisely where it would power his body along the rough hewn track at the roadside to its optimum speed. As if his legs knew before his mind exactly where he was going.

The weather was considerably better, the sun shining its hazy light on the morning mist, which hung low over the loch. Still and silent and foreboding. The stranger looked neither left nor right and seemed unaware of the beauty surrounding him.

Passing Annie's cottage on his left, he skirted the rocky entrance and pressed on to higher ground above the small holding. The land levelled out quite sharply, unseen from the road and cut the mountain backdrop in two, causing a widespread cleft between dark green firs, clinging eagerly to the sloping ground.

At the far end was another cottage. Not as big as Annie's but set at an angle so that a view of the loch was uninterrupted. His purposeful walk soon took him to the property. He stopped. Examined the dwelling in front of him and turned and gazed at the loch below. His eyes betrayed nothing. Still as the loch. Brown as the bark in summer when the light is shut out by the thickly dressed overhang of leaves.

Turning he moved once again to the front door. Old and weather beaten like a boat left out for too long, he pushed against the restraining hinges. There was no latch or lock on the door. It opened fitfully and admitted rays that had not penetrated the interior for years.

The main L-shaped room, encompassing a scullery and bedroom on one side was the sum total of the living space. An unused attic held nothing but bric-a-brac and cobwebbed rubbish piled haphazardly on its beams.

A stone fireplace, filled with rubble that had collapsed over the years, bulged onto the stone flagged floor. Windows front and back were intact but in tone with the rest of the house, useless as light-givers.

Broken furniture littered the floor with what was left of a table and two chairs propping each other up.

Next the man went into the scullery and found a stone sink blocked with plaster from the ceiling and a tap, unused for far too long. Outside, a privy connected to a cesspit provided the only sanitary amenity for the small farm. The man was not interested in that.

About two acres of ground went with the cottage, the estate agent had said. He explained that the low rental was due to the dilapidated state but stressed that it could be made habitable by a good restoration company – the name of which he just happened to have available. The stranger declined and asked for the key to the cottage. There wasn't one.

He stripped off his coat and shirt, revealing well toned muscles that indicated to some extent, the power beneath the six foot frame now shifting rubble and dirt with a shovel and a pick he had found in the shed at the rear.

He worked for ten hours non stop until the place looked almost habitable, with a clean, flat, paved floor, windows that now shone in the morning sunshine, and a grate that gratefully was sucking the hot smoke and flames up its recently swept chimney.

The scullery came in for similar treatment and soon clean water, supplied from a tank sited far up the side of the hill, itself filled regularly by spring water, was smoothly running as it had many years before.

Satisfied with his work, the stranger dressed and closed the front door, placing a lock in the hasp and staple he had fitted, and strode once again back along the loch shoreline past where Annie and Kate were enjoying childhood memories of their schooldays.

They did not see the stranger pass.

Chapter Four

'I hear there's a new chap who's rented the place just around the corner from us,' said Annie, as she came in from the yard with more logs for the fire. 'Moved in last Tuesday by all accounts. Looker too! they say.'

'Haven't you had enough of men?' laughed Kate. 'It can't be more than a couple of years since your last disaster.'

'Never get enough of men. Life's too short. And I've a great libido, or whatever you call it.' The girls both collapsed into giggles and set about tidying the place up.

Kate had asked to go into the nearby town of Tarvie, about three miles south of the loch. Annie was preparing a picnic lunch for them both with a suitable bottle of wine to down the strong cheese and onion sandwiches. 'We can stop on the way back when we've finished our shopping and I'll show you Loch Garve in all its glory.' The way Annie rolled her eyes brought a smile of happiness to Kate's face as she relaxed for the first time since her troubled past.

Annie was quite correct. She hadn't talked about it to anyone who was overly sympathetic and who tried to skirt round the subject whenever it came up. Kate had not had time or the opportunity to dispel all the feelings of disgust and horror that had beset her when the terrible truth came out at the trial. Her husband on trial for murder! A child murder at that. The publicity had almost killed her too. She had thought often of ending it all, to stop the incessant inquisition into her private life with a "pervert." It was as if it was almost her fault. She'd heard the gossip of how she "must have known"or had "condoned it" in some way.

How could she have been so wrong about someone? What deep, unknown traits lay beneath many a "settled marriage?" Could she have urges that had not surfaced yet? Do you suddenly inherit them from some deep underlying quirk in your character that is yet to be awoken?

The end of the trial and the sentence of thirty years had helped. Kate had bravely faced all attempts to get her to give her side of the marriage. Newspapers and the media all wanted their share of the "spoils" of what everyone had called a perfect union.

She had refused and had still been crucified by the press for her "no comment" attitude. But she had ridden the storm and had come out stronger. It still rankled in the night when she had no control over what her brain wanted to live through again. Annie's offer to come to Scotland and "chill out" as she put it, was just what she needed. She already felt calmer and more settled away from the familiar surroundings of where it all happened.

Kate rid herself of her niggling thoughts and concentrated on the present. What the future held was anyone's guess. And who would want to know anyway?

The drive to Tarvie was only fifteen minutes at a slow pace in Annie's van. Packed to the hilt with the items of her trade. Anything that could be sold or exchanged in the various Car Boot Sales she attended throughout the year. Not a great living, but now and then, a handsome profit enabled her to stock up on regular household items in constant demand.

'You're a survivor, did you know that,' observed Kate as she enjoyed the vista of the loch and the far shoreline wedged up against the towering pines and the slate grey mountains thrusting up through the trees. 'Who'd have thought that a High School education would make you into a wheeler/dealer? You didn't even bother with the mock examinations as I recall, but still you managed a fair result when the GCSE's were awarded.'

'It's not the work you put in, it's what you put into the work that counts,' replied Annie. 'Remember the Latin exam?' Without waiting for an answer she explained. 'Six questions of which two were to be answered. Two of those were a translation into Latin from English and a translation into English from Latin. Cinch. I didn't bother with the gerund, grammatical, or subjective and objective rubbish of the other questions. Couldn't have done them anyway. No – Latin is logical and so much a part of our language that it was easier to clog together some sort of sense in both questions. A literal interpretation that seemed in favour with the examiners.'

'As I said. A bloody marvel you are,' said Kate, snatching a glance at her friend wrestling with the steering wheel in the twisting track road she had taken to show off the loch in "all its glory."

'It'll be a bloody marvel if we get there in one piece after the damage the rain did to this track. Most of it's missing.' She wrenched the wheel hard over and finished on the grassy bank just before a gap in the road where it had been washed away. 'Including that bit!'

'Can we get around?' Kate asked.

'Course we can. There's always a way round.' She got out of the car to weigh up the situation.

'Can I help?'

Annie turned. Startled to hear a male voice. A man stood there. Still and waiting for a reply.

'Er ..... well. Er ... I suppose so. We can't get to the other side of the hole without going over the bank and that's too steep for the engine to make it.'

'With a bit of a push, it won't be too difficult.' The man moved to the rear of the van.

Kate got out of the car and raised her eyes to Annie as if to ask if she knew the man. Annie signalled that she didn't.

'Get behind the wheel please. Let off the handbrake when I tell you.' He turned to Kate. 'Perhaps you could lend a hand too?'

Kate was flummoxed. She couldn't stop looking at him. Six feet tall or just over. Black hair swept back into a pony tail overhanging his shoulders and a face of an angel showing perfectly symmetrical lines from his eyes to his mouth. She forced herself to the task in hand. 'Yes. Where would you like me to help?' What a silly question she thought.

'I'll push from the rear if you stand beside me and we'll push the driver's side, there's more weight there.' He turned his attention to Annie. 'Start the engine and put the car in second gear. Release the brake when I say and ease the accelerator gently against the camber of the hill. If the car slips sideways, keep the wheels straight. He took up his position with his back to the double doors at the rear. Kate stood beside him holding on to the outer edge.

Annie started the engine and put the car into second gear as instructed. A shout from the man indicated that she should release the handbrake. She did so.

Slowly the car moved up the incline and levelled out with the road. A heavy grunt came from the rear, but Annie carried on slowly easing the van forward. At the top of the incline she fought shy of turning the wheel inwards as this would allow the van to slip and from the sound of the exertions coming through the window she knew that the man was pushing his legs in a pumping action, similar to the tug-o-war teams she had watched at school sports. With a mighty expulsion of air from gutted lungs, the final shove propelled the van past the gaping hole and the van slid easily down onto the track in front.

Annie stopped and jumped out to thank the man. 'I don't know what we'd have done without you … er …'

'No sweat. The first part was the hardest. Think you'll be OK now.' He started to wend his way down to the loch as Annie shouted. 'Thank you again Mr.… ?'

'Adam,' came the one word reply. Then he was gone through the trees.

'Well. What do you think of that then?' Annie turned to Kate who was searching for signs of the man emerging farther down the hill. There was none.

'It was a dream wasn't it?' said Kate.

'I'd like to be in a dream with him again, you can bank on that.'

'Who was he?' Kate turned to Annie.

'Adam, that's who.' She grinned. 'Probably the original if what I've heard of the first man on earth.'

'Just a bit gorgeous wasn't he?' Kate realised that for the first time in months she had looked at a man and found him attractive. Before then all masculine figures were anathema to her.

'What a start to your holiday though. Just like a fairy story isn't it?'

'I think I have seen him before,' announced Kate.

'You what!? Can't have. You haven't been here two minutes.' Annie turned to look at her companion gazing steadfastly out of the windscreen. 'When?'

'On the journey up here on that ghastly night. In the rain. I thought I saw a man.'

'In that weather?' Annie looked incredulously at the now calm loch.

'Yes.' Kate hesitated. 'Well, I thought a saw a figure. Just like his. Walking along the shore.'

'How far away were you?'

'On the main road above the loch. Probably a hundred yards or so.' As soon as she said it, she knew the reply she would get.

'Well there you are then. Teeming rain, a Scotch mist and a blurry windscreen. How could you tell it was even a man?'

'I don't know. It just seemed like it.' Kate shook her head and threw her arms up. 'Sounds stupid doesn't it? But I saw something.' She relapsed into silence. 'Then how is it I got the same feeling just now when he appeared. I sensed that I had seen him before.'

'In your dreams more likely. I see men like that every night.'

'You're incorrigible. Is that all you can ever think about?'

'Yes. Is there anything else?' Annie collapsed into a peal of giggles and guided the van into a space in the car park.

Kate's thoughts were disturbed continually by the image of the shape on the shore and the man heaving and pushing with taut muscles and whipcord thighs threatening to burst his jeans. She wasn't aware of his thoughts as he toiled. Was he aware of hers?

'We shall have to ask around the town if anyone has seen our handsome stranger. Most likely they will keep it to themselves if they have,' she chortled.

Chapter Five

Craig "Craggy" Stewart had been a feature of the surrounding villages for years. His unkempt appearance and muck ingrained face were familiar to every shop he visited begging for a handout of cash or food. Of indiscriminate age and hunched beneath shiny black trousers and overcoat, no one could tell his height or what shape his body was.

Long, dirty grey hair covered his head. The only relief being the two dark eyes peering through the mess of his fringe. Smoke blackened lips thrusting through the mass of hair covering the lower half of his face were continually licked to wipe away the spittle.

A bulbous nose completed the picture of one of Dickens' typical characters from the poorest parts of London. Craggy didn't come from London. He'd never even left Scotland. He boasted that he was a direct descendant of the famous Stewart clan, but could never prove it. Neither could anyone disprove it.

His cart, purloined from a supermarket, was his sole possession. Sleeping rough and cooking rabbits or rats on an open fire in the forest, he survived on what he could cadge or catch. No one knew how he managed to always have a bottle of some spirit concealed in his greatcoat. Drunk through his tobacco stained lips, it created an aroma that was not pleasant to be nearer than six feet.

He had been lucky today. The butcher had tossed a large ham bone that he usually threw in the bin at the back. It had a meagre amount of meat left on it, but was nectar to Craggy when he roasted it over his fire on an upturned dustbin lid.

The night was calm. A few clouds drifted across the overhanging black curtain of the night, pinpricked with stars. The two potatoes on the lid with the ham bone cracked as they started to burn. Just as Craggy liked them. He leant to scrape the meal onto his tin plate. There was a sound of something moving behind him. Plenty of children had played tricks on him in the past and he was ready for them. He slowly picked up a stout stick lying beside the fire. The end was purposefully left in the embers to ward off anyone disturbing him. He turned swiftly and thrust out his stick, sparkling with the movement in the air.

Nothing was there. Just a quiet rustling of the breeze along the shore of the loch. A soft splash of something in the water. Then a padding sound of a heavy animal approaching. Nothing like he had ever heard before. Suddenly, out of the mist coming to stand before him was a horse. Black as the night and still as an owl. Its eyes were the colour of ebony. Big orbs of black edged with white. They looked at Craggy and bore no malice in them. Craggy was not afraid. He was accustomed to horses from the intermittent horse fairs that visited the district. But this one was different. He had heard of the tales and often related them to the willing tourists who gleaned every morsel of his vivid description. Embellished as he thought fit.

It moved perceptively backwards, nodding its head, inviting Craggy to follow. He was powerless to resist. Forgetting his dinner, Craggy meekly fell in behind the animal, admiring its strong hind quarters and muscular legs. For some reason Craggy measured the distance between him and the horse. He knew what he had to do. When the horse paused, he strode alongside and using a tree stump as a booster, mounted the inviting back.

Craggy was lost in a world not of his making. He rode the horse as if possessed. Impossible to dismount - his legs were glued to the heaving flanks - he clung to the long mane in terror, trying in vain to detach himself from the smooth seal-like skin of the horse. He knew what was to come and screamed to the keepers of the night. They were deaf to his shouts.

The stallion galloped full pelt toward the beckoning loch, plunging in with a crack like thunder as its tail smacked the surface and it was gone taking its rider with it. Within a minute, any sign of a disturbance had abated and the loch stilled once more.

Chapter Six

'So where do you think he's gone then?' Ailsa Morrissey shot the question at the local bartender as she sipped her sweet sherry through age-cracked lips. 'He hasn't been seen for two days now. Not like him.' She shook her head.

'Don't know. Not like him to miss a day begging for a dram. Can't say I missed him yesterday though. Thought one of the other barmen had probably served him.' He returned to drying his glasses and dismissed Ailsa's persistent nosiness.

'Summat's happened to him. Always see him on the road in the mornings, pushing that old cart of his. Nods, then waddles his way into town. Day don't seem right without him around.' The old woman drained her glass and sucked some spittle back through her toothless mouth. 'Go and look for him. That's what I'll do.'

Lives down by the loch toward the south, she mumbled to herself as she walked painfully along the road away from the town. She paused, looking at the still waters. 'What secrets do you hold then, you slumbering bugger?'

She reached a spot where she could look down to where she knew Craggy had his hideaway. A small, self built wooden, tent-like shelter that barely enclosed his feet. She scrambled awkwardly down the rutted path and approached the camp. She noted the ham bone and potatoes, burnt to a crisp on the dustbin lid. No one was in the hideout. The rusting trolley stood incongruously to one side; empty.

The emptiness impressed itself on the whole area and Ailsa knew that Craggy had not spent the night there. Where was he? She would ask around some more.

The fear in her bones would not leave her alone. She tried to dismiss the dark thoughts from her mind, but nothing could shift the image of one of old Craggy's description of his night of terror some two years previously.

'I'll tell ye now,' he ground out as he sipped from his battered flask. 'No matter how I tried not to look at that apparition pounding out of the water, I could'ne. It was like I was transfixed. Unable to move or shout or defend meself.' He shook his head at Ailsa. 'There's many say that I was in one o' my drunken binges, but I was'ne. I remember that I had nae liquor that day. Mean old sods would'ne give me any at the pub.'

Ailsa remembered his eyes, searching even now for any disturbance on the loch. Wild and scared. 'What did ye do then?'

'Nothing. Just stood still and hoped it had'ne seen me. Then it looked straight at me with those big dark black eyes swallowing you up like the bottom of a well. Then it suddenly turned and galloped away through the trees to the top of the loch.' Craggy turned to look at Ailsa. 'Ye ken what happened that night?' He didn't wait for an answer but reminded her of the headlines in the local paper. "Girl disappears from Gorstan."' He paused. 'She was never seen again.'

Ailsa sucked in her breath as she recalled the account related by Craggy. She'd heard tales from her grandparents about mysterious goings on around the loch, but everyone put it down to folk tales invented to keep their children away from the deep water. Unlike the others in the village, Ailsa was sympathetic to Craggy's story. He did not frighten easily.

Perhaps he was in a delusion, but the story was not exclusive to Craggy. Over the years, others had gone missing, not just from this loch, but from Loch Luichart to the west. Ailsa reserved her judgement and searched further along the shore for signs of Craggy. Or the demon he feared.

The shore was hard and rutted. Not likely to leave any footprints or even hoofprints. Ailsa scoured the edges of the water and peered into the shallows for any signs. There were none. She shook her head and swore at the still waters. 'What evil beings do ye hold, ye smitherin', useless blotch on our beautiful countryside.' It was true that the loch did not find favour among the tourists as one of the prettiest in that part of Scotland, and most avoided it. Normally opaque and full of weeds, creating huge areas of a swamp-like surface not accessible by boat or man.

'That does'ne stop whatever it is that haunts the loch,' Ailsa murmured and quickly scurried away to the village. She would keep her thoughts to herself, as no one wanted to listen to the tittle-tattle of a moth-eaten old woman.

Chapter Seven

'Listen Kate. You've been here for over a week now and I've noticed a change in your demeanour. You are more relaxed and a little bloom has come onto your face. God! Sound like a psychiatrist don't I?' Annie poured a white wine for her friend as they sat outside the front door on the beaten old bench, just sufficiently strong enough to hold the two of them.

'I do feel better. Thanks to you. I've begun to think of today rather than dwelling on what the past brought me. As soon as I can remember the past with no dark or disturbing feelings any more I shall know I am on the road to recovery.' She stared out at the loch. 'That's what my doctor said anyway. But you're far better than she is.'

'Thanks. I'll send my bill in at the end of the month.' Annie paused. 'You are stopping 'till the end of the month aren't you?'

'Of course I am. I was told to take anything up to six months if I wanted to. That is the time they reckoned that it would take to get me back to full working condition.' Kate burst into laughter. 'It takes less than that to recondition an old banger doesn't it?'

'Yes, but you're not an old banger - not yet!' Annie dodged the nudge intended for her right arm. 'Hey! Mind my drink!'

'You're right. I do feel better. Appreciating everything around me now, instead of letting it pass as if I had lost the ability to see the world for what it is – unaffected by the pitiful machinations of man. Who could create a beautiful countryside such as this?'

'It's not only the countryside you admire,' said Annie cannily. 'I saw you looking at that Adam the other day. And it wasn't in appreciation of his intellect either.'

Kate jumped. She hadn't realised that she had made her feelings that obvious. 'I was very grateful for the help he gave us. Just because he is knock-dead gorgeous doesn't mean I have to go all gooey eyed over him.'

'But you did. You couldn't help it.' Annie giggled. 'And I couldn't either.'

'Wonder who he is?'

'Dunno. We'll have to find out. Only lives about a quarter of a mile away.' Annie drained her drink. 'We'll pay him a visit.' She raised her eyebrows as Kate appeared to question the intention. 'As neighbours. That's what good neighbours do isn't it?'

'He was rather handsome wasn't he? In a too perfect way wouldn't you say? Everything about him in precise proportion and symmetrically shaped. Balanced and hiding an enormous amount of body strength in those muscles.' Kate suddenly felt quite shy and blushed at her thoughts. She checked them and told herself that she was getting carried away by it all.

'What did you really feel when he was heaving beside you Kate? You've never let me know how you view the male sex now.' Kate didn't reply. 'I mean, you must miss the sex side of your life like I do. But do you yearn for someone, just to remind you what it was like when you first experienced it?'

After a pause Kate spoke slowly. 'I never think of it now. It is dead within me. There is no such thing as perfect sex and longing for it again will only make it more painful. It died in me a long time ago. When I think I used to go to bed with that monster .....' she faltered and put her hand to her mouth .... 'I can never live that down. Never.'

'Of course you can. You have changed your name from MacManus to Grainger. That was a start. You are now as you were before you were married. Single and available.' Annie put her arm around her companion. 'Anyway it wouldn't be kind to deny some worthy bloke the benefit of your charms. All the young chaps around here would die for a date with you.' A mischievous smile cracked her face. 'The only trouble is there are no worthy blokes around here!'

Kate and Annie almost spilt their wine as they rocked together on the bench in fits of merriment. There was a long silence then Kate spoke.

'I wasn't the only one keeping an appreciative eye on our gallant saviour. I saw the lascivious look you kept giving him as the sweat rolled down that superb body of his.'

'You're right. When someone like that suddenly strips in front of you, it conjures up all the old desires. I've still got them even if you say you haven't. I daresay, if you hadn't have been there, I would have made a play for him.' Annie's challenging eyes told Kate that she was deadly serious.

'You mean you would have let him .... you know ...'

'Take me there and then?' A big grin broke out on Annie's face. 'Too bloody true I would. There's not much chance around here of anybody else being up to the job. I like mine strong and silent. And as handsome as that bloody stranger. Perfect sex in my opinion.'

'But how can you enjoy sex without any feeling for the man?'

'Oh, I would have had feelings for him. From the first moment I clapped eyes on him, I got those feelings and he knew it.'

'How do you know that?'

'From the way he stared at me when we were over the hump. Like he'd never had it for some time as well.'

'You're incorrigible. I used to put up with it at school, because I thought you were just playing around with all those lads.' A thought struck her. 'Did you actually let some of them do it?'

'Yes.' Annie looked Kate full in the face. 'All of them.' She nearly choked as she said it. 'Only one at a time of course!'

'What have I let myself in for coming to stay with you?'

'A lot of fun if I have my way lady. Now relax and soak up the atmosphere. I've a notion that it is going to heat up somewhat over the next few weeks. Yippee!' She downed her wine in one go. 'Now when are we going to visit Adam?'

Chapter Eight

Annie loaded up her old Austin van with all the contents of her store cupboard under the stairs. Everything from pots and pans, crockery, toys, clothing, books and ornaments were neatly placed into the positions that they had been previously placed and had come back with the van, unsold.

'Whoever wants all this sort of stuff?' asked Kate.

'You'd be surprised. These days, anything has a value. You never know just who is going to turn up and fancy something on your stall.'

'Now you're talking about Adam again,' joked Kate.

'Now there's a thought. Wonder if he'll turn up? Haven't seen him since he helped us.' She snapped her fingers. 'And we haven't been to see him have we? Could have been waiting for us to drop in for a chat and a thank you and whatever.'

'In your dreams. He's probably forgotten all about it. And us,' said Kate as she opened the passenger door and climbed in. 'Where is this place we are going to?'

'About twenty or so miles in a small village on the other side of the ridge at the back of us. A lot of people make the journey. It's like a fete day. Food, music, stalls, a fairground, and us of course. It's what we Scots call Hogmoney.' Annie kept a straight face as she waited for Kate's reproach at her outrageous statement. She wasn't disappointed.

'First of all you are not a Scot. Secondly the word is Hogmanay and that's held on New Year's Eve.' Kate turned and saw Annie's cheeky face bubbling with laughter at her friend's seriousness. 'I wonder sometimes how you ever managed to get any GCSEs at all.' Still trying to keep a straight face she realised that it was hopeless and the cab was filled with two females chortling all the way to the fair.

'How much for that then lass?' The tall, gawky individual bending over the table pointed at one of Annie's vases.

'How much do you think it's worth?' said Annie.

'Probably a lot less than you.'

'You'd be right there my old cocker. Tell you what I'll do. I'll let you have it for tenner more than I paid for it. That's not much of a profit for me, but I'm feeling generous today and you look like you really fancy it.' Annie stood back and watched the gangly man's face.

'Aye, I'll give ye that, but ye have'ne given me a price yet.'

'Fifty five quid.' Annie gauged the silence between them. 'I could get twice that in Edinburgh you know.'

'Aye,' the man said again. 'But they dinne know the value of anything.' He pursed his lips. 'Tell ye what. I'll give ye fifty and that's my last offer.'

'God you drive a hard bargain you Scots.' There was a pause. 'OK. Fifty quid it is. Not much in it for me, but as I say, I'm in a generous mood today.' She took the money offered and wrapped the vase in newspaper before handing it to the man. 'Take care now. Don't tell any of your friends what you paid for it. It'll ruin me.'

Kate had watched it all from behind the stall. 'Was it really worth all that?'

'No. It was a copy that I picked up myself from a stall two weeks ago. Looked good and it had all the right marks on the bottom. Cost me a fiver. Good buy that.'

Kate held her sides as she gasped in disbelief. 'You've swindled that man and you didn't turn a hair.'

'What's wrong with that? He's happy, I'm happy. The person I bought it from was happy. Everybody is happy. That's what it's all about.' Annie turned to her next customer with a smile as warm as the sun creeping over the trees behind her.

Kate watched as the crowd increased until near lunchtime. There was very little room on the car park for any more vehicles. Country life. That is what Annie had been trying to tell her about. Not the city hustle and bustle, where everyone knew no-one and scuttled to and from work each day not noticing anything of the world around them. Here there was time. Time to appreciate all that nature gave to this precious earth. Including its inhabitants. Where they all behaved like adults.

Her eye caught sight of a dark head in the distance. Smooth and perfectly groomed, standing out above the melee of folks after a bargain. It moved slowly among the various stalls, stopping now and then and disappearing from view. Then it re-appeared and moved closer. Kate held her breath. It was him wasn't it? How did she know that? One short meeting over a week ago and his face and physique were still in her mind. Annie was right. He had awoken something in her that she had long forsaken. She turned away, busying herself with re-arranging the items on her part of the stall. Annie was busy too.

When Kate turned again in the direction of the smooth black head, it had gone. Confused, she was spoken to rather sharply by a shabby little man who wanted to know the price of the jumper on display at the back of the stall. 'Er .... I think ...'

'Well come on then. How much is it you blitherin' Sassenach?'

Annie caught the gist of the raised voices and came to Kate's rescue. 'It's too much for the likes of you, you old varmint. And that's a Sassenach's word for piss off.'

The man retreated swiftly through the crowd that was honing on to the little spat.

'You have a way with words don't you?'

Annie looked up at the man with shiny black hair and a dimple on each cheek. 'I was taught well,' she replied, not sure if he was giving her a compliment or not.

'I like a woman with balls. Not many of them around these parts. Men are too much in the ways of the forefathers.' He chuckled. 'Sassenach eh? I gather you're English then?'

Annie drew herself up to her full height of five foot one inch. 'Aye, I am, to borrow a Scottish word. And proud of it.'

'Good for you. A mixing of the blood is good for both nations. Hope our contribution was a good match.'

Annie felt slightly deflated in being reminded of her errant husband. 'He didn't do much for Scottish morality if that's what you mean. He buggered off six months ago.'

'I'm sorry to hear that,' the man said. 'A complete misjudgement on his part I would say. There aren't many good women to choose from these days.' He touched his forelock in the old fashioned way. 'Hope you have better luck with the next.'

As he walked away Annie shouted after him. 'What makes you think there will be a next!?'

Kate was relieved that the man she thought might be Adam had turned out to be someone else. Or was she?

'Annie,' she shouted to her friend. 'When did you say that we were going to visit Adam?'

Chapter Nine

Something disturbed the restless sleep that Kate was having. Creaks and groans from the uncertain masonry of the cottage; the east wind funnelling under the eaves; strange cries from unknown animals; all had contributed to a variety of reasons why she couldn't sleep. But there was something else. Something that was in her subconscious that was troubling her.

After the trial of her husband Angus MacManus, she had been bombarded with both sympathy and scorn. The latter bothered her most. How could some people connect her with what he had done? Maybe it was pumped up by the media who never lost an opportunity for a story that was never there but which could be fed until enough of the population began to believe the unimaginable. That she was part of it!

This was normal, she had been told. But was it? Should she have known? How could she sleep with a man and not know his innermost thoughts? But she had.

Countless times she had run her marriage through her mind, trying to pick out little clues of what she had let herself in for. A great courtship, a quiet wedding with few guests, Angus's family being marooned in Scotland, or so he had said. Her own reduced to a few friends as her parents had died when she was young.

It was inevitable that they would pair up, both working in the same environment and often together. It was almost endemic in the police force to marry "in house" as very few outsiders would ever understand their collective affinity to their colleagues.

Although she had been warned of the dangers of too close a relationship in work, she had overridden the prejudices and married her fair haired suitor. At just under six feet, well built and athletic – he played for the police rugby team – he was the ideal husband. Several of her fellow policewomen secretly envied her, she could tell. His hair gave a pale tint of red in certain lights, leading to him being christened 'Ginger MacManus.'

Kate remembered the lonely nights when he would come in late from some survey or other of suspects. As these become more regular, she had actually plucked up the nerve to enquire discreetly about the force's work on these occasions and what surveillance was being carried out. Several times she had learnt that no such surveillance had occurred on a particular night.

When challenged innocently on the subject, Angus had dismissed it as "one of the secrets of his special work and not officially logged at headquarters."

What a fool I was, Kate admonished herself as she sat up in bed looking out at the full moon over the loch. Me, a detective or so called, and I couldn't even have recognised what was on my doorstep. No wonder the population were in two minds as to whether she was involved.

The only redeeming feature was that she had been instrumental in bringing him to justice. Tracking him night after night until she caught him enticing a young girl into his police panda car.

Radioing for help she had confronted him and freed the young girl before he had hit her and kicked her in a rage she had never seen before. His green eyes ablaze with anger and spite as he shouted his frustration to the wife at his feet. Again and again he kicked until one vicious boot caught the side of her head and she lost consciousness.

Battered and bruised, she had related her story to the Manchester detectives who subsequently found too many discrepancies in Angus's statements. He maintained that he had no sexual relationship with Kate and that he was out of his mind that night, not knowing what he was doing. It was all her fault, he said. The detectives thought otherwise and connected him with the dates and times of the disappearance of two young girls over the past four months. He denied everything but the evidence against him was complete when a witness came forward to say that he had rented a garage to the man some nine months previously.

It was taken apart and the brick floor removed to reveal the bodies of the two young girls.

Wall shackles, tinned food and a water source were in evidence. Angus MacManus had no defence left. Despite his protestations that it was nothing to do with him, he was sentenced to be retained during her majesty's pleasure with a minimum of thirty years before parole could be considered. Many thought the sentence was too lenient, including Kate, and said so.

The fuss died down, Kate tried to return to work and forget her ordeal but was sent on extended sick leave after four months back on the job. Angus was already settled into his life at Strangeways Jail in Manchester.

Not again, thought Kate. I can't go through all these memories time and time again. I have to rid myself of the nightmare.

It was true that when she thought of the past it did not make her a nervous wreck any more. Angus was safely put away. She had a new name. No one knew of her new identity, not even the police officially. She would tell them when she eventually returned to work. If she did.

The moon beamed down onto her bedstead, lighting up the myriad of square colours that Annie had hand sewn from bits of material gathered in her search for stock items. Red and blue, purple and green all blended together into a wonderful melange of hues that helped to calm her nerves after the initial shock of remembering again.

From her vantage point she could see the border of the loch glinting in the moonlight. Like the edging of a glass table. Almost as bright as day, yet with that translucent quality that hides the imagery in its folds. As still as a photo shot. Unreal. Ready for the front of a chocolate box.

Something moved. Kate peered through squinting eyes. Nothing.

There it was again. Moving slowly south as though on a slow boat. A figure. But a figure of what?

Then for one brilliant moment when the moon cleared the smeared glassiness of its reflections on the water, the figure emerged. Naked and loping easily along the shore almost as if his legs were wheels. And it was a he, Kate observed. Although the figure had his back to her, she knew that no woman had a physique like that. Only one person she knew matched the quality of the back and hard buttocks now displayed in vivid contrast to the waters behind him. Adam.

Chapter Ten

'I have some bad news for you MacManus.' The Governor of Stangeways spoke with little sympathy or facial expression as he looked up at the prisoner standing before him. 'Your mother died early this morning.'

Angus MacManus didn't re-act at first. Then his lips trembled and he swept his fair hair back from his forehead, covering his eyes with his hands. He shook a little and the guard standing beside him stepped forward a pace. The Governor stopped him with a shake of his head.

'How … how … did she die?' Angus at last managed to stammer.

'Heart attack, I am told,' said the Governor. 'Five o'clock this morning, in the A and E at Hope Hospital. Neighbour telephoned the ambulance when she found her slumped against her door late last night. That's all the details I have.' He paused for a moment. 'Sorry.'

Angus nodded, wiped the tears from his cheeks and asked what happens now.

'The funeral has to be fixed of course. After the post mortem. Should be in about a week.'

'Will I be allowed to go?'

'You will have to apply. It will be a matter for the Board. As you are a category one prisoner, it will not be likely that you will be released to attend. That is all.'

Angus turned and made his way back to his cell. He had plans to make. And the first one was to convince the Board that he genuinely wanted to be at the funeral. It was imperative that they regarded him as a reformed character and completely devastated by his mother's death. He knew he could pull it off. He had put on pretences like this many times in the past to avert people's suspicions but this one had to be the best.

He cried continuously for some two hours, refusing to go to meals and recreation periods. His regular attendance at the gymnasium was missed – he was the keenest of all the inmates, honing his body to a fitness he had never attained on the outside.

He continued the sobs at night, much to the annoyance of neighbouring cells and they all complained to the warders, who in turn relayed the message to the Governor.

The meeting of the Board took place four days later. The post mortem had been completed and the funeral fixed for two days hence. Angus MacManus was summoned.

'First of all may I express my sympathy for your mother's death,' said the chairman.

Angus nodded. Couldn't give a sod he thought to himself, but was pleased that the chairman had looked closely at the red patches around his eyes and his gaunt appearance. Four days of rubbing dust around the eye sockets and eating little or no food had created a picture of someone who had been deeply affected by the death.

'Thank you,' he muttered.

'Given the seriousness of the crimes for which you were found guilty, it is not normally the practice of the board to allow any licence to prisoners no matter what the reason.' The chairman glanced at the remainder of the Board who remained non-committal. 'However, there still remains the question of compassion for someone in your situation. The loss of a mother is monumental and we believe that it would be inhuman to deny you the right to say your farewell. In the circumstances and bearing in mind your impeccable behaviour since your incarceration, permission is granted under the usual terms of day release for prisoners in your category.'

By the greatest act of control Angus MacManus did not move a muscle. His heart and his head were pounding in triumph. Now he'd show the bastards! Two days to plan it all. That would be no problem. He had been working on it for four days already. The fine details would be honed to perfection and then he would be free.

There were very few mourners at the Roman Catholic Church of St. Mary in the suburbs of Gorton, Manchester. The church Angus had attended from the day he was old enough to walk. His mother and father had instilled into him the catholic faith and he had even been part of the choir for a while. Small and routinely set out with a central aisle and a high altar. To one side was the confessional box. A set of three doors allowing access to a small vestibule which connected to its twin by an intricate fretwork framed window. Angus had used it many times. His sins always being forgiven by a generous father leaving him free to commit more.

The service was brief and without too much ceremony, Angus was handcuffed to his guard on the hard wooden pew. A second officer sat beside him at the back of the church. He put his minder through as much trouble as he could with his constant kneeling and prayers and wiping of his eyes, so that the guard's arm was like an extra tentacle being manipulated at will.

The service over, Angus stayed to kneel for a final prayer. He rose and shook his head, overcome with emotion. 'Bye Mum,' he sobbed. 'I'll say a prayer for you every night.'

The guard stood like a spare part not knowing whether to join in the grief or tug the prisoner away. Angus spoke. 'Do you think I could just say a word to the father? Confess my sins. God knows I've got enough of them.' A sort of Irish charm wormed its way into his speech, something that he had discarded long ago, but found useful on occasion to charm others.

The guard did not move. Angus spoke again with more fervour in his voice. 'It's probably the last time I shall be able to speak to Father Donachie. He has been my counsellor since I was knee high to a grasshopper.' He applied his most sorrowful look and almost broke down again. 'Please.' He used all his persuasive tone to emphasise his misery.

The guard spoke. 'I suppose that would be in order. As long as you're quick. The van's waiting.'

I know, thought Angus as they went toward the confessional box. Angus opened the door to the middle one. He knew that one. He had played in it as a lad. He knew all its secrets.

'Could you call Father Donachie for me?' Angus held up his handcuffs. 'I can't really do penance with these on can I? You're a Catholic aren't you? It wouldn't be right would it?'

My guess was right when they allotted Patrick O'Neil as my chaperon. A Catholic. One element in his favour. Religions stick together don't they? Especially the Catholics. Like blood brothers. Angus's anguished judgement of his jailer strengthened his pitiful plea.

Patrick O'Neil hesitated. He had been to enough confessionals to appreciate the importance to the confessor. He couldn't go anywhere could he? He would be stuck in that box wouldn't he? 'We'll be right outside. Be quick.' He signalled for his colleague to join him.

'Thank you. It means so much to me.' It is all the difference between captivity and freedom you burke, thought Angus as he slipped into the box.

The fretwork came away in his hand under a little pressure as he knew it would. A joke they had played on the father many times.

Father O'Neil sat on his side and immediately remarked on the missing fretwork. 'Still up to your tricks Angus MacManus?' He shook his head sadly. That was the last thing he did in life as Angus reached through and clamped his neck in the crook of his arm and wrenched it to one side. The regular lessons in the gymnasium had strengthened his muscles so that it was relatively easy to break the spindly neck of his parish priest. All the time he kept up a mumble of words to cover any sounds he made.

A quickly executed exit to the other side was accomplished with further mutterings and Father Patrick's body re-instated in a sitting position as before. Dipping down below the eyeline of the boxes Angus slipped quietly into the vestry where he knew a private door led to the churchyard. Once across the barren and forlorn surroundings, a simple jump over the stone wall and he was free.

Walking at a pace that would not attract attention he looked for a likely car. There was always one available; he knew that from his time on the beat. A small window open, even an unlocked door. They were common and he did not have to search for long.

The drawer to one of the desks in the vestry had supplied him with a screwdriver he needed. Another remnant of his memory of what the church stocked.

One sharp insertion of the screwdriver through the side window and he could push it down and reach the lock. In! Now for the wires behind the starter key on the dashboard. You learn a lot in the police, enough to make a career out of being a villain, he chortled.

The car, a Ford Cortina, jumped into life and he moved swiftly away from the back street and juggled his route to avoid any of the main streets until he was far enough away to relax and head for the M60 to join the M56 on his way to Altrincham. There he had a rented garage, the one the police never found. In it was all he needed to put his next plan into action.

In between Altrincham and Bowdon was a spare piece of land on which someone, years ago, had built a block of four garages. These were advertised locally and Angus had snapped up one for a peppercorn rent in a false name. It was his secret hideaway. In one corner was a large four-drawer steel bureau bearing the usual security lock at the top. At the back of the second drawer, which Angus removed, was a strong box on its side. The original drawer had been shortened to hide the depth. He extracted £50,000 from the bundles of notes in the packed box and a handgun. He fondled the easy handle and pulled the clip containing seven bullets from its socket and shot it home again with a satisfying click. Rescued from a raid that had gone wrong when one of his fellow officers dropped it, he had never returned it. Could come in useful some day he had reflected. And so it had. The Walther PPK .380 calibre gun, a favourite with the squad because of its size – just 6.1 inches long and weighing only 22.4 ounces, it fitted perfectly inside a jacket pocket.

Next he turned to the lower drawer where he had a spare suit, shirt and tie and decent shoes. The prison garb was discarded in a plastic carrier bag. A further box revealed a kit with false moustache, beard, wig and stage make up. He chose a small bottle of dye and a pair of horn rimmed spectacles that would complete the transformation and he would bet that his own mother wouldn't recognise him. She wouldn't recognise him where she was now he laughed.

A short trip along the A556 to the nearest garage where he filled up and asked the attendant for directions to the M6 Southbound access point.

'Straight on mate. Can't miss it. About four miles.' As he gave Angus his change he asked. 'Going far then?'

'Far enough. London's a long way and I don't fancy the journey through Birmingham.'

'Best o' luck mate. Rather you than me.'

'Thanks.' Angus made sure that he gave the attendant a good look at him and the car parked near the pump. 'Don't know if that old banger will make it. These old Fords are a bit unreliable.'

He drove off in the direction of the motorway, then made a right turn at the roundabout towards Lymm, a quiet little town but with another grotty garage tucked away at the side of the lake. There; after he had removed the number plates, he ditched the car deep into a gully covered with trees and shrubs so that it practically disappeared from view.

Tomorrow he would buy a cheap car from the dealer, who he knew was not too choosy about his customers as long as they had the cash.

Tonight he would bed down in a disused shack behind an empty factory, another refuge from the world of the law.

As he made himself comfortable on a few straw-filled sacks his thoughts turned to the one who had been the main instrument of his incarceration. 'Sleep well bitch. "Revenge is mine saith the Lord"' he quoted. 'But mine will be sweeter.'

Chapter Eleven

Adam's place was set back from the road into a flat area between two hills further up the loch side. It reached deep into the highlands until the slopes took over again and enclosed it in a three sided shield of rising pine trees, oaks, and chestnut trees. The soil was good. It had been allowed to deteriorate over the years with no occupants to instil any life into it. Until Adam.

All around the cottage had been junk. Dumped as it became useless and allowed to form some sort of modernist sculptor's idea of an alien landscape. Adam had rescued a host of iron railings, an old bedstead and an ornate fireguard. In the stone blast furnace, created in the hillside from rescued rocks, his bellows blasted the fire to white heat and enabled him to create a plowshare, a scarifier, and tiller. These were extensively used to churn up the overgrown two acre plot and return it to its arable state for a harvest of mangels beside a blackberry hedge, whose flowers of lilac, pink and white had turned into a bountiful harvest of fruit. Wheat was also on his agenda and a spare plot for fast growing cabbages.

Set to one side was a small paddock, surrounded by attractive half logs cut from some sturdy trees that he had felled and shaped with a power saw, resurrected from the equipment in the barn. At the back of the paddock was a brand new stable for two horses. Logs intertwined and filled with pitch from the loch bottom, they would have graced any Laird's holding of thoroughbreds.

Finished hoeing between the rows of mangels, Adam turned his attention to the fruit trees, expertly pruned and now producing a plethora of buds boding well for the autumn market in apples, pears, and plums..

The weather was turning out to be far better than expected with a warm climate that begged the plants to burst through the rich soil into the sunlight. Row upon row of lettuce and carrots filled what remaining space he had in the cottage garden. Behind them stood the current bushes, already green-berried in their eagerness to soften and shine.

That was the sight that met Annie and Kate as they drove the battered van up the rutted track to park in front of the smart, newly painted front door. A proud brass knocker invited them to announce their arrival and Annie did not disappoint. Four loud raps echoed in the rooms behind the door. There was no answer. Annie motioned for Kate to follow her around the house.

Their astonishment at the change in the land nearly took their breath away. Everywhere was producing something. From the tiny herb garden adjacent to the back wall to the towering fruit trees in the far distance. Annie's gaze took in the new stable about a hundred yards on the right. Kate's was fastened on the figure coming toward them in an easy stroll.

'Hello,' said Annie.

'Hello,' came the reply.

'Thought we'd just drop in to say thank you.'

'There was no need.' He continued to walk to the back door.

'But you helped us out of a mess and we didn't have time to show our gratitude,' explained Annie. 'So we brought you these. Didn't really know what you would like, but the colour will brighten any room.' She held out a large bunch of delphiniums picked from the hills at the side of her garden.

'Very kind.' He stopped at the door and took the flowers.

They stared at each other for what seemed an age, then finally he said. 'Would you like to come in?'

Annie needed no further prompting and Kate reluctantly followed.

Adam looked at Kate and she felt a deep penetration of his unwavering eyes. She didn't feel uncomfortable, but it was not easy to fathom out what he was thinking. She brushed her dark brown hair away from her brow and almost skipped past him into the kitchen.

Annie was amazed at the difference a clean and a redecoration could do to what had been a total mess. She'd been in once about two years ago and wondered why no one had demolished the place. It was that near to a dump that it wouldn't have taken much effort.

'What a beautiful kitchen. Did you do all this?' Annie turned to Adam.

'Yes.'

'It must have taken a lot of effort. And time,' she added.

'Not too much if you keep at it.' Adam took an old but clean kettle and set it on the wood burning grate to boil. 'I can offer you a cup of tea if you want.'

Annie looked at Kate. Their eyes were asking the same question with no answer. Who was this monosyllabic man who apparently showed no emotion or eagerness to chat to his neighbours?

'No sugar, just milk please.'

'Same for me,' echoed Kate.

Adam set three mugs on the polished wood table and neatly poured three steaming measures into the vessels. A drop of milk and spoons were offered.

Again the women expressed their thanks.

Having finished their drink the three stood awkwardly, Kate and Annie not knowing if they should stay or try to see the rest of the cottage. Annie had an idea. 'I suppose you have transformed the rest of the cottage too?'

'Yes.'

Annie decided to be impertinent. 'Could we see it please? I love these kind of cottages and it might give me ideas for my own. It's only a quarter mile or so from this one, but I never seem to have the time to do any DIY.'

'This way.'

They followed him into the small inner hallway, itself a neat square of whitewashed walls with a hall stand and a vase and pictures on each side. Kate noticed the pictures were of animals and birds.

A highly polished oak door opened into the front parlour, as Annie was to call it later. Scatter rugs of rough wool covered the tiled floor and two easy chairs sat each side of the arched stone fireplace. Again a rosy glow of hot pine wood radiated to every corner of the room.

'This is beautiful. A lot different to when I saw it last,' said Annie, revealing the fact that she had been nosing around before his time.

'I like it.' That was the first indication of any sense of pride that Adam had expressed.

'And the land at the rear. However did you manage to clear that?' Kate was vainly trying to evoke some sort of conversation. And no doubt his fondness for the life he was leading would almost force him to speak of his efforts. Again he looked deep into Kate's eyes and almost communicated his thoughts without speaking.

'I had the help of my two horses. I could not have done it without them.'

Annie remembered the stables. 'So they're in the stables are they?'

'No. I let them out in the daytime to wander as they will among the trees. They do not go far, the slope is too angled for them to climb to the top.'

For the first time, the women saw a semblance of pride of ownership. They took their leave, thanking Adam again and promised to drop in later in the month, if he wouldn't mind.

'No,' he said.

'You can, of course, visit us anytime you're passing. You know where we live. Out most of the day but you'll be welcome after five any night. That's when we return after our hard day's toil on the markets.'

Adam lifted his head and nodded. They exited the front door, noting the small bedroom to one side. Adam had an afterthought. 'I might need odds and ends for the house. I believe you have a selection?'

Annie couldn't wait to get into the van before she chortled to herself and nudged her companion. 'How about that then? Every girl's dream. A handsome bloke, a place fit for a queen, and a business that I know is going to thrive.'

Kate agreed. Her thoughts were still on the night she had seen Adam on the shore of the loch. Hiding a blush as she recalled the stark nakedness sparkling in the moonlight and the rush of adrenalin that she had almost forgotten existed.

Chapter Twelve

Valuable contact has been made with those living nearby. The community is gradually beginning to accept our presence.

Good. Caution is required at all times, remember that. Suspicions run deep and it will be difficult to allay fears if the truth be known.

Two females have visited and appear to be level headed. One particularly has a dark secret to hide. There is a sense of it when she is quiet. It creates a magnetism that reaches out and disturbs the natural aura.

These are natural feelings among those you associate with now. You should not be tempted to follow the inclinations now emerging. It is not time yet. There are far more important matters to attend to. We shall tell you when we need your help. In the meantime, keep your council and do not do anything to alter the way the community feels about your presence.

Chapter Thirteen

'Who's that at the door?'

'How should I know,' said Annie. 'Open it and you'll find out.'

Kate did as Annie asked and took a little step back as she was confronted with the uniform of a police constable. Only this one had shiny gaiters and a motorcycle helmet.

'Yes, can I help you?' Kate immediately felt a fool as it was obvious that he had called to elicit some sort of help from them, otherwise why would he be there?

'Yes, ma'am. If I could have a few words with you and Annie McBride. I'm investigating the disappearance or non-appearance if you like of Craig Stewart.'

'I'm sorry, won't you come in?' Kate hurriedly stood to one side to let him pass.

Annie came down the stairs and met them in the sitting room. 'Hello Joe,' she said. 'Bit off your patch isn't it?'

'Aye. But you know how it is, the whole force is short-handed and I've drawn the short straw. But it's all the better for seeing you again.'

Kate raised her eyebrows at Annie in a "what's all that about then?" sort of query.

'This is police constable Joe Murray. He's stationed at Dingwall but covers most of the highland around here.' She turned to Joe. 'And this is my very good friend Kate Grainger. She's here on holiday.'

'Pleased to meet you I'm sure,' said the young man. His eyes took in the dark fall of Kate's hair and the way it framed her heart-shaped face. Kate was aware of his scrutiny.

'Not looking for a criminal here are you?' she joked.

'Not that I'm aware of,' he smiled. 'No, it was Ailsa Morrisey who first raised the question as to where old Craggy had gone. He appeared to be too well known around the district to disappear for long. She tells me that she has been to his camp and it shows signs of being deserted. Not like old Craggy she said.'

'And what can we do for you then?' asked Annie, sitting on the arm of her sofa and showing the young man a smooth expanse of leg.

'Well, I thought,' began the constable, distracted by the leg, 'I thought that you could give me some background information, seeing as how you overlook the area where he had his haunt.' He sat down as he got a nod from Annie that he should do so.

'There's not a lot I can tell you that you don't know already. He has been here ever since I moved in – over two years ago. Called now and then for a handout of anything we could spare. A loaf of bread, matches, bacon, fruit. Anything like that. Harmless old coot. Had some weird tales to tell when he felt in the mood.'

'Oh, and what would they be then?' He took his notebook from his breast pocket and penned something on the page.

'Oh he had hundreds of them. Most of them about the war – not that anyone believed his stories of his heroics in the Royal Navy. Said he had served on submarines.' Annie laughed. 'Still, you could never catch him out with dates or battles or the like.' She shook her head. 'I liked him.'

'And you er ... Miss? Grainger.'

'Ms. Been married. Now divorced,' said Kate anticipating his question.

'I'm sorry.'

'I'm not.'

'Did you see anything suspicious in the last few weeks before he disappeared?' Constable Murray returned to his notebook.

Annie thought. 'No; nothing more than usual. I saw him probably three times a week ago, trailing that old supermarket trolley into town. He looked as normal as he always has. Mind you, that isn't the normal we apply to "normal" people. But everyone accepts his scruffy and filthy appearance. Anyone would look like that if they lived in his conditions.'

'And how long have you been here Ms Grainger?'

'Kate please. I've been here oh, ... so many weeks I can't remember now.'

'And have you seen anything out of the ordinary?' His eyes again took in the symmetry of her face as if he were measuring the details.

'Well, I ... we ... I mean.' Kate looked at Annie. 'I thought I saw something odd on the journey here .....' Annie's lips pressed together in a warning not to get into fantasy.

'And what was that then?' His gaze never left her face.

He's quite good, thought Kate. His technique was by the book.

'Oh, there was a storm and the visibility wasn't good, and well, I thought I saw someone running along the shore of the loch..... and then there was a horse ... and then it vanished.'

Annie emitted a loud "Hah!" and fell into the sofa. 'If you hadn't been stone cold sober I'd have said that you'd had a wee dram or two.'

'Well, perhaps the conditions did create some sort of illusion. I don't know.' She covered her embarrassment with a deft sweep of her hair over her head. The constable's stare remained for a fraction longer than necessary.

'And what do you do Ms … er Kate?'

'What do I .. oh .. er.. I'm a freelance writer.' Kate returned his stare until he glanced down at what he had written.

The constable turned to Annie once again. 'Could you take me to where his hideout is? I understand that it is not far from here. You must almost overlook it from the road.'

'Yes. I know where it is. Haven't been there for some time. Don't get the opportunity these days with a full day's work seven days a week.' She fetched her hat and coat. 'Would you like to go now?'

'If you've the time, aye. I gather we'll have to walk.'

'Well we can't go on that bike of yours. But you could give me lift sometime when you're passing. I've fond memories of pillion riding. It's fun!' She laughed uproariously. 'Especially with a handsome bloke on the front.'

Kate laughed with her and caught the rather embarrassed look on Joe's face as they exited the cottage.

'Freelance writer! That's a good one that is,' said Annie, nudging Kate as they followed Joe Murray out of the front gate and over the road to the slope leading down to the loch.

'Hope we come across your naked runner! See what the constable makes of that!' Annie skipped down the path like a six year old. 'Wait for me Joe. There could be a murderer on the prowl!'

Chapter Fourteen

He'd done it! Angus congratulated himself on fooling the police. He listened to the one o'clock news on the car radio. Reports were flooding in from all directions as to where the escaped murderer was heading for. If at all. Some said he was lying low. Some said he had reached London in a stolen car, others just floundered in the lack of progress.

Detective Inspector Clare Baddeley sat in her office surveying the fiasco that yesterday's events had produced. Two police escorts, one prisoner, a visit to a funeral resulting in the biggest manhunt for over twenty years. Both of the offending officers had had their bollocking from the Chief and were subject to prolonged questioning from a range of detectives who showed no sympathy for their plight. "A right load of muck they've dropped the force into," and other less polite comments were bandied about.

DI Baddeley brushed her fair hair back behind her ears. Although now over forty, she retained the look of a woman just holding onto her youth. Fit and slender, the regular sessions at the gym testified to that, her frame sat neatly on the plush leather chair behind the huge teak desk dominating the small room.

She re-read the details. "Departed Strangeways jail 1140. Two escorts, prisoner handcuffed to PC Brian Coleman.

Second escort David Summerbee accompanied, sitting beside the driver of the Mercedes car. All doors were locked as per routine. The journey to the Church of St Mary, Gorton was uneventful. A small congregation was present. The two PCs entered the church and sat on the back pew to the left with the prisoner between them.

After the service, prisoner Angus MacManus had asked to take confession. After consultation with each other, the PCs agreed. The handcuffs were removed so that Angus MacManus could enter the confessional box. Both PCs stood close to the door of the confessional box. They heard the quiet mumblings from the box for some minutes until there was quiet. On opening the door they discovered that the box was empty while on the other side they could see through the opening that Father Donachie was dead. His neck was broken. A search of the other side of the row of confessional boxes revealed that Angus MacManus had disappeared. Probably through the back door of the vestry.

A white Ford Cortina had been reported missing from nearby. There were no other indications of where Angus MacManus had gone.

It is assumed that he escaped in the Ford and enquiries of local residents were fruitless.

The language, as taken down by a junior WPC was stilted and basic. What had been an audacious and cunning escape was whittled down to a mere jumble of facts blurted out by the two PCs when questioned individually. There was a tendency for each to blame the other, or the hierarchy for having no set down procedure for Roman Catholic prisoners.

Despite the instruction that on no account were the handcuffs to be removed, they had been, albeit for a religious rite that conflicted with the main police constable's own conscience.

'So much for them,' muttered DI Baddeley. What to do next? She had been presented with the conundrum immediately she had reported for duty on being summoned on her telephone.

'Find him,' was the brief command from her Chief. 'There will be hell to play if we don't and I will be joining the condemnation of a force that at the moment is not fit for duty.'

Clare pursed her carefully lipsticked lips and plotted the time scale.

Escaped from church – 1325 hours. Car reported stolen – 1405. Forty minutes or so to clear the immediate area and get to where? Search for the car instigated 1410 and co-ordinated with all police cars in an area of twenty miles in the first instance. Sightings, enquiries of CCTV cameras on motorways, main roads, town centres were set up. These would take time and might not show results.

One break came an hour later as a Panda Car phoned in that a garage on the A556 had reported a white Cortina buying petrol. The attendant particularly remembered the man and the car as they had chatted about the trip to London. His description of the man matched that of Angus MacManus even down to the touch of ginger on the top of his head. He had driven away in the direction of the M6 motorway.

Clare again pursed her lips. If he had gone to London, there should be video footage of him from several of the M6 cameras. But she demurred immediately taking as gospel the evidence before her. The film may or may not show the Cortina. As one old detective had advised her many times. "Always look beyond the obvious. And always remember to take into account the person you are chasing."

She turned her attention to the file on DI Angus MacManus. Rapid promotion, good results, and a reputation for hard line approach to criminals. Lots of minor successes, but a marked lack of the "big movers" of the city. Known throughout the criminal world, his contacts had produced valuable files on ongoing cases. Some reservations were noted in that he was always in the forefront of the news. Very few of his colleagues would denounce him, but neither would they express approval of his methods.

There was no evidence of any wrongdoing, but Angus MacManus kept his associations close to his chest and didn't let any assistant pry too closely into his connections with the underworld.

A bit of a lad about town, was one description. Smart clothes, expensive wristwatch, and a new car every year did not add up to a middle of the road detective. Clare knew exactly how she had to budget to exist. How did he afford the extras? "My old man left me loads when he died," was his boast. Then why was he in the police force? "Just for the sheer hell of it," was his retort.

Clare did not like Angus MacManus. She had never liked him, but had known plenty like him in her twenty five years of service. They existed. They were tolerated. They eventually slipped up. As Angus had. She read the report of his crimes. They disgusted her and confirmed her fears when first reading his CV.

His wife, Katherine MacManus had been instrumental in his capture and subsequent conviction. A man like that would never forgive the treachery of his wife. She noted it down on her pad.

She also noted down the area where the car had been reported and looked on the A to Z to familiarise herself with the district. Not far from the M6, but she would bet her next month's salary that he hadn't gone that way. Too obvious. A deliberate set-up where he knew that the police would eventually find trace of him and his car. So which way had he gone?

The north was the obvious route, towards Altrincham the biggest town from the garage.

What was there? He needed clothes, money, another car, food.

DI Baddeley summoned her assistant DS Jean Cropper. 'I want a team set up to contact every car dealer in the county, covering the area between the M56 and the M62. We are after a cash purchase yesterday or today.' The Detective Sergeant hurried off to start the survey.

If he needed cash, then he must have a place where he keeps it. His bank account had been frozen, there was only the usual monthly income and outgoings of a normal account and a search of his house had produced no other trace of accounts at the time of his arrest. His wife had confirmed that as far as she knew there were no other accounts. But he always seemed to have money. So where was this "load of inheritance money" then?

He was on the take. She was certain of that. Hence he had it stashed away somewhere. Another house? No. That would attract attention. A lock-up. Clare sent for DS Cropper again. 'Another search. All lock-ups in the same area. Landlords' names, renters' names, how long rented for, all the usual details. Description of persons renting if you can get them. And I want it done tout de suite.' She smiled as she saw the look of apprehension on DS Cropper's face. Yes my lady I've been through it all before. It's called police work, she smiled.

Chapter Fifteen

For some reason Kate was restless. She told herself that it was the aftermath of the ordeal she had undergone. But surely I should be over it by now? she reasoned. Perhaps not. The psychologist had told her it would take "time". How long was time?

She rose and walked to the window. A pretty feature set into the tiled roof with a glorious view of the loch and the surrounding mountains. In the dim light, the loch fared better than in broad daylight, its shimmering surface on the far side hiding the drudge and weed gathered near to the slope from the main road.

There was just a suggestion of a moon, which failed in its attempt to break through the dark clouds. To Kate's left was the upper end of the loch following the path of the A835 north. To her right, the loch disappeared into the lowlands and into the Rogie Falls.

Shadows fanned the loch edge, swirled by the dancing branches of overhanging trees. The air seemed heavy through the open window. Signs of another storm like the one when she arrived. She peered at the spot where she had first thought she saw a figure. No one believed her but she couldn't dismiss it from her mind.

Perhaps she was staring too hard, but her eyes misted slightly and lost focus. Something was coming from the southern end of the loch as if on wheels. She could hear no sound and the shape was unclear. But it was some sort mirage growing and shrinking in the dark, blending in with the shrubbery and gorse, sometimes tall, other times small. Then she caught a bobbing movement and tried to associate it with what she had seen before. Then it stopped. Still as a statue. It was almost invisible and at that moment Kate convinced herself that she had imagined the whole scenario and turned to get into bed. For some unknown reason she stopped; looked over her shoulder once more and saw the man. More distinct than what she had seen earlier as it was coming from the opposite direction. It stopped just where the thing had been. Its arm rose to shoulder height and moved gently against the shadows.

Kate was transfixed as she watched spellbound. Was this another illusion? How could she fix it in her mind? Should she fetch Annie? No. By the time she awoke, it would have gone and she would be the butt of more jokes.

The second shape stepped back and turned, now facing north and toward the desperate attempts of the moon to break the cloud cover. A tiny sliver of light filtered down to catch the surface of the loch behind the figure now moving steadily along the path. For one millisecond Kate had a full view of the thing. A man. Naked. Moving in a smooth, effortless motion. Then he was gone. But Kate had seen enough. Good job Annie wasn't here, she almost chuckled. The sight of the finely honed chest and tight stomach, to say nothing of what lay below, would have had her shouting her head off as if she were in a women's strip club.

Nevertheless Kate thought about waking her friend now and relating the whole story before she forgot the details. But she never would forget a scene such as the one she witnessed. Who was it? She had her suspicions but was determined to find out. She had been too long on her convalescence. She needed action. Tomorrow she would begin. First with the old lady Annie had mentioned. She was the most likely one around here to know what was what, as Kate's mother used to say. Annie could wait a while.

Chapter Sixteen

Angus MacManus carefully inserted the key into the front door, shading the movement with his body. It was evening and the street lights were about to come on. Kingsway to the south of Manchester was a busy main road with this section sporting two side roads parallel to the highway. It would be difficult for anyone on the opposite side to notice anything suspicious from that distance and he was hidden from neighbours by the porch over the door.

He chuckled as he let himself into the house he once shared with his wife. Always keep one trick up your sleeve was his motto, and the hidden key in a tin box buried near the drainpipe was his secret.

The house had been empty almost since he was convicted. Kate had moved out to avoid all the accusations and nosiness of the public. It had been empty ever since.

There was an air of neglect pervading the rooms. As if the house had been condemned and left to its own devices. Most of the furniture remained. Angus made for the bureau in his study. Lots of paperwork, reference notes, and private contacts littered his filing slots. He was looking for Kate's friends. Most were those she had met in the force. Very few "outsiders" palled up with coppers, he reflected.

There was nothing to link Kate with any other person who might want to take her in following her near breakdown.

He congratulated himself on still having the nous to work as a detective. How easy is it to find your own wife? Consult the Manchester Police station. It was a doddle. One telephone call pretending to be an anxious associate of Kate's and wanting to have a private word with her "as she had always told me to contact her should I still have concerns over my wife's lover" had really convinced the rookie that his call was genuine.

"If I could just have a word with her, it would be very helpful."

"She's not here at the moment," came the tentative reply.

"Perhaps you can tell me when she will be on duty then?"

"Well .... not for a while yet." The young woman receptionist was still uncertain.

"Look. I used to ring her at home in Burnage, but I can't get a reply."

"No. She left there ages ago."

"Where did she go, do you know?" Angus paused. "I only need her number, she was so much of a help last time I spoke to her." He was getting more confident now. He had the girl wavering with his persistence.

"Her new number is no use to you, I believe she went away."

Bingo! Angus had hit the jackpot. "I don't blame her after all that has happened. Poor girl. Must have gone out of her mind."

"Well, she did take a lot of sick leave."

Even better he thought. "I suppose she went to stay with a friend. Wouldn't be much of a rest in a hotel would it? You wouldn't happen to know if she did would you?"

"No. Not really. She left her address with the office according to regulations. But they're confidential."

"I understand. Quite right too. Thank you so much, you've been very helpful. I'll try her friends that she mentioned. Most of them work at your place, so that wouldn't be any good would it? There was one other she used to talk about. Annie, I think her name was, moved up north somewhere and appeared to lose contact. I wouldn't have thought that she'd go that far."

"I haven't been here long, but Kate did talk about someone in Scotland I think it was. That could be the one."

"Ah well,' sighed Angus. "Guess I'll have to wait until she returns."

"I would leave it for some months if I were you. She was advised to take a long recuperation, poor girl."

Poor girl! She'll be all the poorer when I get to her. "Thanks love. Bye."

Chapter Seventeen

'You're very remote up here aren't you,' observed Kate as she busied herself getting Sunday breakfast of a full plate of bacon, eggs, tomatoes and mushrooms.

'I like it that way. Nobody ever bothers you and you don't bother them. It's a way of life up here.' Annie carried the plates through to the sitting room which doubled as a dining room at the rear.

'No, I mean, you don't get newspapers, you don't have television, and as far as I can see, you don't have radio. How do you keep contact with the outside world?' Kate looked helplessly at Annie.

'I don't. What little news I do hear, I get on my rounds. The local pub in the town, or from the television in the newsagents. Why should I bother trying to get it first hand?' Annie cocked her head. 'Tea?'

'Yes please. But news is part of life. Without it you are a hermit, unaware of the big world around you.'

'Is that a bad thing? From what I hear, the TV is all about convincing you that you need something that you probably don't, rubbishy programmes about irrelevant subjects, and generally brainwashing you into thinking that you can't do without it.' Annie sat down and looked at Kate quizzically. 'Anything you are missing then?'

'Yes. For all I know, the world has stopped and we are the only ones left alive.' She joined Annie in devouring the sumptuous ingredients, cooked to perfection.

'Tell you what. As it's Sunday we'll go into town, have a beer or two and watch what little TV we can. When we've been depressed enough by the news, we can have a run up to the other loch on the other side of the main road. That one is much more beautiful. An artist's paradise, they call it. Loch Luichart. Goes on for miles. Has quite a history too.'

'Oh, what's that then?'

'I'll tell you on the way.'

Loch Luichart was all that Annie had said it was. The scenery took Kate's breath away. From the glittering expanse of water practically beaming in the afternoon sun, to the weathered mountains, covered with firs and lichen encrusted pines.

As deep as anyone could imagine, Annie said that no one had fathomed the bottom yet.

As they sat on the grassy bank with the picnic that Annie had prepared, toasting their long and now renewed friendship with a glass of Chardonnay, they were, as Annie put it, "On a plane that transcends all current problems, unaffected by the trivialities of man."

'That's quite a quotation from you, you know. I wouldn't have thought you thought quite as deeply as that.' Kate looked at her friend with admiration.

'Oh, there's a lot about me you don't know. Remember I was very good in the English classes. A straight A I got.'

'That's about the only subject that you took any interest in as I remember,' observed Kate. 'Except the boys that is.'

Annie punched Kate playfully and resumed her gaze at the loch.

After a while she turned to Kate and said. 'Do you want to hear a story about this loch? One that many people around here will not repeat, or even acknowledge exists. The only person you will hear it from is old Ailsa Morrisey, and she doesn't divulge it very often.'

Kate's curiosity was aroused. She had heard of multiple folk tales connected with Scotland, but had never paid much heed to them, interesting though they were. 'Tell me. Then I'll decide whether you're telling me old wives' tales or not. Most of them are aren't they?'

Annie's expression was serious. 'This is no wives' tale. The folk I know who believe it are intelligent and discerning individuals. People always want evidence don't they? But there are some things that you just cannot dismiss.'

'Stop eulogising and get on with it. I'm all ears.'

Annie destroyed the moment by quipping, 'then your mother should have pinned them back when you were young.'

Both fell about laughing until their sides ached.

'Tell you what Kate. I'll leave it until we can corner Ailsa Morrisey. She'll tell it like it is. She's lived with it all her life. It'll be better coming from her.'

'OK. Let's go into a big town. I've missed the hustle and bustle of Manchester, the people, the shops and everything that goes with it.' Kate packed up the picnic and loaded it into Annie's van. 'I fancy a bit of shopping don't you?'

'The nearest town of any size is Achnasheen, about twelve miles from here. A few shops, a pub and post office and a bakery where we can buy some fresh bread and cakes to take home.'

'Gorgeous! New places always interest me. Lead on Macduff!'

'The names McBride, but like you I'm thinking of changing it. Too many bad memories.' Annie crashed the gear into first as if she was thrusting her spite at those bad memories.

Achnasheen was smaller than Kate had imagined, but big enough to instil a sense of people about their business. The dialect was foreign to Kate and she had to consult continually with Annie as to what was being said to her. 'You'll soon pick up the lingo,' laughed Annie. 'Look at me. No one can tell I'm not Scottish can they?'

'I had a job telling you were English at school. That Manchester accent of yours was shocking.' Kate hurried to a dress shop, the first she'd seen in weeks. As they came out and turned to the town centre, they popped into a newsagents to catch up on the news, although Annie wasn't interested.

Kate chose the top Scottish newspaper and scanned the headlines. Nothing other than current political debate and the ongoing eighties recession that was hitting the shopkeepers all over the country. Turning to the second page the black, double size leader jumped out at her and she gasped and almost collapsed.

"CHILD KILLER AND RAPIST ESCAPES FROM JAIL."

Under the headline, Angus MacManus's picture stared out at her like some horror story come to haunt her again.

Chapter Eighteen

Adam gazed out at the mountains to his left as he sat on the rear seat of the coach heading for Dingwall. The only noticeable large town within striking distance of Loch Garve and set on mainly lowland to the south of Easter Ross and to the north of the great inlet from the North sea, Cromarty Firth.

His research into the archives of the small library in Gorstan has given him the address he wanted. A recognised gunsmith that supplied the local gentry and a fair proportion of the community with the firearms they required. Stag hunting and rabbits and wildfowl shooting were all popular sports and attracted overseas visitors to the glorious grouse shoots and deer hunting renowned throughout the world.

His mission was not to indulge in the so called sport, but to acquire a certain rifle that most suited his purpose.

The shop had confirmed on the telephone that they indeed could obtain the rifle of his choice, but it would be a matter of weeks before the order could be fulfilled. Now the letter advising him of the receipt of the rifle lay snugly in his inside pocket along with the required funds.

He had to see it for himself and test it for the capability that he knew had to be precise.

The journey was uneventful, with few people getting on and none getting off. The driver carefully manipulating the old bus around the winding road as if the bus knew the route better than he.

Adam thought about the last few weeks. He had practically finished his refurbishment of the small farm and was well on his way to being self sufficient in many food items. The crop of wheat would soon be ready for harvest as would the mangels. These would provide a handy income from the demanding market around the district. He had heard the murmurs around the town of how he had transformed the place that everyone had condemned as hopeless. That should have given him a thrill but the compliments went unacknowledged. He soon attracted a reputation of "withdrawn and unresponsive." Not that it bothered him; his feelings were irrelevant, if indeed he did have any. People were people and opinions were of no import to him. He was not used to the banter or the ribaldry of normal everyday conversation. Another term he had regularly heard was "a loner." If that meant keeping himself to himself, then so be it. He did not see any advantage in pandering to the likes of mostly nosy neighbours. They had nothing to add to his lifestyle. He volunteered nothing to theirs.

Except the two ladies. They had struck a chord in him that he did not understand. A sort of affinity between him and them. Different somehow. He tried to figure it out as he had never met this before. He made a mental note to ask his advisers.

The darker one had something to hide. His perception was too finely honed to ignore that something in her past haunted her. She appeared relaxed now but underneath ran a dark current that threatened to disturb the apparent calm that she assumed.

Annie McBride was completely different. Nothing appeared to phase her. Energetic and vivacious, she had also infiltrated his indifference to others. A kind of lift in his stomach and a slight quickening of his breathing he had not experienced before. Something like the feeling when he viewed his acres and a satisfied thrill ran through his body.

The scenery was magnificent. The passing hills in the distance a contrast to the flatland on either side of the coach. Eventually it pulled into a small square overlooked by a typical Scottish church and a tented market extending to all sides. He marvelled at the horde of customers eager to get a bargain before someone else. It puzzled him. He patted the money in his pocket and strode through the crowds to the far side where a row of shops peeked over the tarpaulins of the stalls.

Passing by one of the number of public houses in the row, he was almost butted into the road by a flying body hitting him in the chest. The man fell to the ground in front of him. Adam stooped and lifted the man to his feet again. Suddenly the man's eyes, glazed with the amount of whisky he had consumed, focussed on Adam and with a great roar of rage, lashed out. Adam caught his fist in his and grabbed his other arm before the man could retaliate. Try as he might, the man was held so tightly that his eyes watered and a gasp of pain squeezed from his drooling mouth. All the onlookers turned their attention to the man holding the drunkard in a vice-like grip. Not until the man's rage subsided did Adam let him go. There was no attempt to lash out again, and the man slunk away, fists tucked under his armpits to alleviate the pain.

Some of the crowd knew the assailant and marvelled at the ease with which Adam had held him. "Long time since anyone has done that to Jock" and "about time he got his come-uppance." They looked with respect at the stranger as he resumed his walk to the shop sporting a rifle over the front window.

'What are you going to use the gun for sir?' said the shopkeeper.

'Target practice mostly,' replied Adam.

'A bit pricey for that isn't it?' The shopkeeper was intrigued by the sight of Adam weighing the gun and peering down its sights.

'I like the best,' was all Adam said.

'That's one of the best that Winchester made. 7.62mm calibre bolt action, with a 24" barrel for a flat trajectory and accuracy. It also has a very mild recoil.'

'2960 feet per second I believe,' said Adam.

'Yes sir. You certainly know your guns.'

'And the ammunition?'

'A complementary box is supplied with the gun.'

'Thank you.' Adam replaced the gun in its box, handed over the money and left the shop.

His next call was at the local Police Station to request the licence. There was no problem. Nothing registered against him and his name and address noted in their records.

'Good hunting sir,' said the officer. 'Should manage quite a few with that I should think.'

Chapter Nineteen

The Police Panda car passed him as Angus sat in a lay-by thinking about his next move. He knew that he had to be extra careful. Detective Inspector Baddeley was no fool. He had worked with her and admired her analytical mind. But if he knew her better than she knew him, then he could anticipate her plans and throw her on the wrong track.

Firstly, he was positive that the theft of the Ford Cortina would be associated with him. A search would be instigated, but called off when no trace showed on the traffic cameras. She would anticipate that he had changed it for another. Where? would be her next question. A run down of all the known "cash dealers" would be made and probably a trace of several would be followed up. Even now his number plate would be on police records of all patrol cars. Again he had to change his transport.

It was necessary anyway, as he couldn't afford to book in anywhere for lodgings. His profile was too prominent in the news. Everyone was looking for him. A £20,000 reward by the Daily Chronicle was being made but with his newly applied dye and spectacles, it would be difficult to identify the fair to ginger haired ex copper on the run.

More importantly, where had Kate got to? She was not at home; that was obvious. Living with someone else? If so, who? She had some associates in the force, but none that he could recall would house her. No, the receptionist at the station had given him a fair idea, that Kate was not locally situated. Gone away for the good of her health, was the message he got. If so, where would that be? There was only one reliable friend that Kate had ever talked about – Annie McBride, her bosom pal from her schooldays.

Since Annie had moved to Scotland, Kate had kept in touch and had been genuinely disappointed that the "dream elopement" had gone to pieces. 'Serve her right, the damn fool,' Angus had said. 'Always think more than twice about a lark like that. Too young by half.'

Kate had written to her and asked her to come and stay for a while. She had rejected the idea, saying that she had plans to move somewhere else. His family did not want her now, and she was looking for a place of her own.

The odd postcard had arrived from time to time, with Annie getting more and more settled into the way of life she was living, wherever that was.

Only one way to find out. Find those postcards. Might give a clue as to her location. It was worth another trip to his old home. The heat would be off now around that area, DI Baddeley having satisfied herself that he wouldn't be fool enough to visit the house, which had no doubt been put under close supervision since his escape. It is amazing how many prisoners go back to their old haunts reflected Angus. Attracted by the thought of familiarity, when in reality, it was the most obvious first move the police would anticipate.

With his disguise, and the coast comparatively clear, he could slip in again and root out those old postcards – supposing that Kate had kept them. Perhaps one of the early letters would give him a starting point. Andy's parents' house. They could tell him where Annie had moved to.

Smudging some dirt over the number plates, he drove steadily towards Manchester on the main Chester Road. There was a lot of traffic, most going to the derby between

United and City. Flags and scarves and horns being tooted all along the carriageway would deflect any would be police observation, even if they had located the number of his car.

Making his way across Manchester, leaving the howling mob to live out their dreams or otherwise, he approached the Kingsway from the south, driving through Handforth and Styal. The main thoroughfare was again full of northbound football traffic and Angus was thankful for the cover.

He picked up a black briefcase from the back seat and walked directly to the house as if he had an appointment. He had, but with no one inside, there wouldn't be anyone to shut the door on him.

The key in his pocket inconspicuously slid into the lock. It turned easily and he was in, after pretending that he had every right to enter.

Once inside, he stopped. Where had he not looked before? Every drawer in the bedroom, the bureau, the kitchen drawers and paper racks, the cupboards in the lounge – all had been thoroughly examined. But he had not investigated the loft. As with most houses, there was a lot of junk up there, and boxes of old papers and documents from years back.

Angus smiled. Got to be there!

He fetched a chair from the bedroom and stood it underneath the trapdoor to the loft. Heaving himself up through the opening he sat on the boarded portion and switched on the light. He started sorting the boxes.

I didn't take him long to find Kate's particular store of old correspondence, birthday cards, and old photographs. One of Annie stood out as she smiled with the other 100 or so girls at the photographer. Kate was next to her, beautiful even then. But not now, he thought as he brushed aside his immediate feelings and delved into the bottom of the box.

Among the photographs he found what he was looking for. A postcard from Scotland showing a panoramic view of Loch Ness. It was sent not long after Annie arrived in

Scotland. No address, no date. Another postcard showed six pictorial views of Scotland from the West coast to the East coast. Six lochs beginning with Loch Maree; one of the biggest in all Scotland, Loch Croisg, Loch Fannich, Loch Luichart, Loch Garve, and Loch Glass.

Angus remembered Kate talking about Annie's fascination with the nearby loch but no name had ever been mentioned. But it was a start. He put the postcards into his pocket and searched for any letters which could give him more of a clue. There were none.

Angus was pretty certain that Annie had not branched out too far west as he recalled that her description of the journey after the wedding had taken seven hours just to get to Edinburgh. That suggested the destination was not west. Of the lochs shown only four were possibilities. The first two were too far west, the third a possibility, but the remainder more likely.

He left the house with a renewed purpose of finding the despicable wife who had betrayed him and thinking about the revenge he would take when that day came.

The most important action now was to swap his car again for something more purposeful, now that he had set his sights on Scotland. A camper van would be ideal.

That was soon accomplished as he ditched the present car in the centre of Manchester in a car disposal dump. He didn't think the owners would object to one additional car for crunching that day. That would be the end of the trail as far as the police were concerned.

A plain, light blue flat fronted camper van was easily purchased. A false name and address from one of his shady friends in Manchester satisfied the dealer and Angus was on his way north, complete with accommodation, cooking facilities, and the innocence of a plain tourist on an adventure.

Perhaps there might be other pickings on the way Angus smiled to himself.

Chapter Twenty

It didn't take long for Annie to contact Ailsa Morrisey. When she approached the stall on a cold, wet miserable morning, Annie asked her if she had got any further in her search for Craggy Stewart. The answer was a negative. 'No bugger wants to know,' she moaned. 'As far as the police are concerned he has just gone away.'

'I'm sorry to hear that,' said Annie. 'I always liked old Craggy. I miss him.'

'Something's happened to him. I know it. Not like him to disappear like a jackrabbit. He's been nobbled somehow. I know it.'

'Listen Ailsa. My friend and I are as concerned as you are. We would like to take a look at his camp site. See if anything shows …'

'I've already been there …..'

'I know that Ailsa,' butted in Annie not telling of their prior visit, 'but my friend is an investigative journalist and may see things that we mortals cannot.' Annie put on her best assurance attitude that she was in earnest. 'It wouldn't do any harm would it?' she pressed, seeing the look of doubt spring into Ailsa's eyes.

The old woman paused a while and then nodded. 'S'pose it wouldn't. Three pairs of eyes are better than one anyway.' She turned and walked away.

Annie shouted after her. 'Can we go tomorrow morning? Meet you on the road outside of my house. OK?'

The old lady raised her arm above her head signalling a yes, or so Annie surmised.

Ailsa knocked on the door of Annie's cottage just as she and Kate were finishing their breakfast. Refusing the cup of tea that Annie offered, Ailsa signalled that she was eager to be on her way.

Kate and Annie bundled themselves up in winter-warm duffel coats and woolly hats and trailed after as fast as they could. Ailsa was no slowcoach and forged ahead to the break in the hedge where feet of the hikers had created a natural gap. From there, the track led downwards towards the loch glowering in the early light.

Annie had never liked the expanse of water even though it was considered a tourists' attraction. The only problem was that very few of them ever came this way.

The air to Annie always seemed like ice whether it was winter or summer. From the flat grey loch, came the quiet quenching of cold instilling in her mind the need for a sharp dram of brandy.

Today was no different. No birds tottered along the shore. None flew overhead. There was an absence of song in the air. Kate noticed it too, but said nothing as they ploughed through the thickets that were eager to fill the pathway.

Ailsa paused. Sniffed the air and started again. 'Gonna rain,' she said. Annie agreed. Sullen skies crowded the mountain tops, as if shielding them from the sun. They hurried on.

'He used this camp for the past few years. I used to come and visit in the old days, but it got too much for me.' Annie pointed to a gap in the trees that hugged the shore.

'Wouldn't get me sleeping anywhere near this loch. Too much of a temptation.'

'What do you mean "temptation?"' Kate saw the look of dread in the old woman's eyes.

'Not for me; for them.' She pronounced.

'Them?'

'Aye. Them that lives down there.' Ailsa pointed a crooked finger at the far side of the loch.

Before Kate could take the conversation any further, Ailsa pushed aside some brushwood and led them into a clearing. Shaded on all sides by the sharp needled pines, it was an ideal hideaway for a recluse like Craggy.

'That's his home.' Both Annie and Kate stared at the homemade shelter and the basic cooking utensils made from scrap. Particularly at the upturned dustbin lid that had been used for Craggy's last meal. Or so it seemed.

The bone still lay on the lid, blackened and covered in ash blown up from his "grate."

What few possession he owned stood around the site. Particularly his trolley, which he had never been seen without. It was said, recalled Ailsa, that he got a new one every year from the local supermarket in exchange for not hanging around the place.

'Looks like he was disturbed,' said Annie.

'Aye,' repeated Ailsa. 'Or something disturbed him.'

'What could disturb him here?' Kate again caught the look of fear in Ailsa's gaze. 'What sort of wildlife do you have in these parts?'

'No wolves now. No other beasts of that size. Just the normal forest animals. Rabbits, hares, moles, rats. A few foxes and o'course, sometimes we get a stray deer from the other side.'

Ailsa was hiding something, Kate was certain of it. 'You mentioned temptation when we got here. Who or what would be tempted by Craggy's presence?'

'Don't know. Always left him alone till now. Sort of respect you know. He knew them and they knew him. Can't understand it.' Ailsa rumbled on to herself as if she were alone.

Annie looked at Kate with the same perplexed expression.

'Tell us what you mean Ailsa. We can see that Craggy has gone from here. What makes you think that he hasn't just shifted his abode?' Annie faced Ailsa across the empty plot.

'Examine the ground. You can just see where he walked to the water's edge. Must have been muddy that night. It meets the water and then stops.'

'That merely indicates that he started paddling along the shore,' said Kate. But she went nevertheless for a closer look. The shoe prints were faint but still there. There was a gap and then the sign of hoof prints. 'Something else was here,' she said turning to Ailsa.

'Aye. It were one o' them.'

'What?' Annie suddenly had a daunting feeling in the pit of her stomach.

'A Kelpie.'

Annie gasped as she heard the dreaded word. She had been told in hushed tones a few times of the myth that refused to be discredited. Most never talked about it, as if to mention the very word would bring the associated doom on them.

'A Kelpie?' queried Kate. 'What's that?'

'Nothing you would like to meet young woman. Better to keep yoursel' to yoursel' and mind your back.' Ailsa scurried off the way they had come.

Kate turned to Annie, whose face had turned an ashen colour under the dark woolly hat. 'What exactly is a Kelpie?'

Chapter Twenty One

Adam stood in the stable block admiring his work as the two jet black perfectly groomed horses reflected the light jutting in from the open top door. Both were immaculate and appeared to preen their pleasure in their appearance.

With coats like a seal just out of the sea, as smooth as finely tanned leather, they could have been carved from polished ivory.

Their eyes met Adam's and held him in a secret conversation. Words were unnecessary when ideas floated from one to another. He knew they were pleased. They commented on his progress with his purchases and with the contacts he had made with those around him.

We feel the time is nearing when you will have the opportunity to carry out your task. The one you want has moved from his former home into the Loch Garve area and is setting up home at the north end. He has already scouted around the shores for likely prey and we feel sure he will strike soon. He is a maverick and must not be tolerated. Ever since the council evolved from the previously held indigenous beliefs, he is the only one who rejected the new order. We must move forward and to accomplish that you will have to be resolute in your mind that all must be destroyed who participated in the former culture.

Adam understood the instructions perfectly. The past tense brought home to him the choice that would be denied him. It worried him that it would mean the destruction of some entities very dear to him. He did not want to face that but the conditions of his being where he was now did not excuse any deviation from the goal he had been set.

I am ready to do your bidding and will not fail to carry out the task to its fullest extent.

The two pairs of dark brown eyes gave their approval of his commitment and his devotion to them. They knew he would not fail in the duty they had set him.

Chapter Twenty Two

Angus chortled to himself as he hurtled around the twisting roads leading to the highlands. Edinburgh had been a doddle, with multiple traffic in and out of the city, giving him cover if he needed it. No one had challenged him. No one was following him.

They were all sitting in their pitiful little offices trying to outguess his moves. Futile and with little guidance from any of the enquiries they had made. No doubt they had traced the car dealer and had a description of the vehicle he had purchased. Too late. It was now an undistinguishable lump of crushed metal in a Picasso type pile of junk.

The first port of call after he had familiarised himself with the terrain, was the McBride household. Somewhere north of Edinburgh, but where in this vast expanse of peopleless country only fit for cattle, deer, and wild animals? Rain in all its misery had shown him the dismal, perpetually soaked forests and hills, that photographers avoided with their glorious sunshine tinted pictures of "glorious Scotland."

'Bloody heathens,' Angus muttered as he swerved to avoid yet another deep rut in the road. He pulled over to consult his map. He had left Loch Ness far behind and was approaching the Moray Firth. Surely there must be a large town where he could start his enquiries, examine electoral lists, housing lists, or at least learn where he could find them.

Having made his decision to carry on north, he looked for somewhere to eat and rest after a gruelling drive of almost seven hours. A small hamlet broke the boring two sided forest alleyway that had accompanied him for the past four miles. At last. A sign of life. A public house – Campbell Arms – presented its welcome face to the passing trade. Parking at the rear of the pub, Angus made his way through the back door.

'Guid day to ye sir,' said the landlord, or so Angus surmised.

'Good day.' Angus looked around the lounge. No other person was present.

'What'll ye have?'

'Make mine a pint of your best ale please.' Angus was always up to the niceties of polite conversation. It gained you a foothold in new contacts and formed the first pleasantry.

'Travelled far?' asked the landlord as he deftly pulled the foaming ale from his ornate pump.

'Far enough,' said Angus.

'Not fit to drive in this weather.' He tried again. 'Where are ye heading then?'

'North to the lochs.' Angus decided to ask his own question. 'I'm looking for an old friend of mine from my younger days. Name of McBride. Called himself Jock, but that could have been a nickname. Lived up here somewhere. Near one of the lochs I believe.' Angus had deliberately chosen "Jock" as he was unaware of the Christian name.

'McBride eh?' The landlord scratched his thinning hair. 'No-one o' that name around these parts. You could try the wee shop up the road. It doubles as a post office and they would have a better knowledge of names than me.'

'Thanks. I'll do that.' Angus finished his pint and left.

On his way to the shop he saw a trail of schoolchildren, accompanied by a teacher walking on the footpath. His pulse quickened and he eyed them for far longer than he should. Time for that later, he thought.

The post office was more of a help than the pub when he told them that he believed the man was a baker. Angus vaguely remembered the occupation when Annie wrote to Kate. The Postmistress, if that was what she was, looked it up in the yellow pages and found that such a business "McBride's Bakery Co." was being run in Strathpeffer, a small community at the junction of the Cromarty and the Moray Firths.

'Aye that'll be the one,' the fussily dressed assistant said, peering through her thick spectacles at the gentleman standing on the other side of the counter. 'No other bakers around these parts with that name as far as I know.'

'Very good of you I'm sure. How far would that be then?'

The woman cocked her head to one side showing the beginning of wrinkles around her neck and calculated slowly. 'No mor'an ten miles I'd say.'

'Thanks very much for your help.' Angus almost touched his forelock, but smiled his winning smile at the impressionable shopkeeper.

On his way back to his van, his thoughts turned again to the trail of children clutching their satchels and looking very innocent. Just how I like them, he thought.

Time to bed down in his van and lay low for a while. Plenty of time for the McBrides in the next few days. He was in no hurry.

He sat back contentedly on the lounger in the camper and let his mind wander over all the possibilities that had suddenly presented themselves.

Where and how would he claim his prize?

Chapter Twenty Three

'You haven't explained what that woman Ailsa meant when she said "Kelpie." Kate sat opposite Annie in the small lounge drinking their morning coffee. 'And why is everyone around here so frightened to admit they know what it is. Even you,' Kate added as Annie bit her lip.

'It's something that has been handed down over the generations, getting more and more implausible each time the tale is told. I myself was told it by Andy's parents. Real died in the wool Scots they are. I didn't believe it then and I don't now.'

'What don't you believe?'

'The fairy tale that is part of the culture around here. Probably started as a ruse to attract visitors, but it must have backfired, because not very many come, and when they do, no one will talk to them about the myth.' Annie shrugged. 'And it is a myth, I'm convinced of it.'

'If it's a myth, why don't people talk about it?'

'That's the funny part of it. If they don't talk about it, they think it will never happen to them.'

Kate was getting exasperated now and put it to Annie. 'Start from the beginning and tell me all you know about this myth, this Kelpie thing. I'll not tell anyone else so you will be safe with me.' A half smile broke out on Kate's face as she faced her friend.

Annie took a deep breath. 'I'll tell you what I know. Or what I've been told.' She finished her coffee and sat back in the armchair. 'It is said that in Loch Garve, there exists a supernatural water horse – no don't interrupt,' Annie said as Kate tried to butt in. 'It is in the shape of a normal horse, immensely strong. Most are black, though some are white. It appears as a lost pony with a coat like that of a seal but icy to the touch. It lures people, especially children into the water and consumes them.' Annie saw that Kate was entranced. 'Now this is the fascinating bit. They can transform themselves into human form to attract people, then when they return to their horse shape they invite the person to ride on their back. Once on, they cannot get off and are lost forever.'

Kate sat stunned. 'And you are telling me that the majority of people around here believe all that?' She laughed, then asked a question. 'How many people that you know have disappeared from around here?'

Annie had to admit that she knew of only one. Craggy Stewart. And it wasn't yet established that he had vanished.

'When we went to his camp yesterday and with Joe beforehand, there were signs that he left in a hurry. Food on his cooker. His trolley was there, footprints leading to the water. But that doesn't mean he was taken by this … this .. Kelpie thing.' Kate waited for a response.

Annie almost seemed ashamed to doubt her friend's analysis, but still had doubts about what had happened to Craggy. 'Maybe. But if what they say is true, then perhaps there is a Kelpie in the loch.' She jumped up and went into the hall. 'Tell you what. Let's go and see someone who I believe has first hand knowledge of this legend. Old Jackie Brewer. Lives about six miles to the south of the loch. His family have been associated with this myth for donkey's years. His stories are so outrageous that in the end he almost convinced everybody that it was all in his head. But …'

'But what?'

'See what you think of him, then I'll tell you another story that I was told when I first got here.'

The short journey to Jackie Brewer's house was driven in silence, both lost in their own private thoughts. Annie still believed deep down that there was something in the myth; Kate withholding her judgement like a true copper until she had positive proof. Or as near as she could get.

The news of Angus's escape had dislodged her temporarily, but a resolve that she thought she'd lost, came to her aid and she had talked of the consequences to Annie quite openly. He had escaped. He did not know where she was. He did not know her new name. No one at her old station would divulge any information. Or shouldn't. Knowing how details did slip out, she was concerned that Angus, with his knowledge of police procedure, would eventually find out she had gone away.

But forewarned is forearmed, she consoled herself. She knew his habits and his faults. Nevertheless she would seek help in defending herself. For some unknown reason, she thought of Adam. Perhaps it was his indefatigable manner that impressed on her that he would be a match for any assailant. Silly, she scolded herself. I hardly know him. Still … he might come in handy.

'Penny for your thoughts madam,' said Annie.

'Oh … nothing. Just reviewing my options I suppose.'

'It's that bugger Angus isn't it? Worried are you?'

'A bit. But I am sure I can cope with him, if he ever comes near me.' Kate sounded more sure than she felt.

'We need a guardian angel, that's what we need,' said Annie.

'I know you'll think me silly, but I've already thought of one…..'

'Adam,' said Annie in unison with Kate.

'He does have that effect on you doesn't he,' laughed Kate.' A thought struck her. 'Do you know, I never saw him blush or look embarrassed. Stoic type I reckon.'

Annie pulled into the gravel front garden of Jackie Brewer's house. A stone built two-storey structure with blue slate roof and mullion windows. It looked as dead as the rocky screed behind it.

Several knocks on the door brought no response. They went down the side of the house to the half window framed back door. A loud rap on that and they saw signs of movement.

A voice shouted from a room not visible to them. 'What do you want?'

'We'd like to talk to you Jackie. Remember me? Annie McBride? You're the one who told me about my husband?'

There was no answer. 'I'm not here about him though. I have a friend who is a journalist and wants some first hand information that only you have.'

Kate nudged Annie and whispered, 'journalist?'

'Shush. I think he's coming.'

The door opened and a small wizened man with a balding head and long sideburns beckoned them in.

He walked with a peculiar gait and his arms were permanently bent as in most old men.

'Sit ye down.'

Annie and Kate sat side by side on what could loosely be called a sofa.

'What do ye want to know then?' His voice was like old cardboard left out in the rain. 'I've told it all before and nobody believed me.'

'I did,' stated Annie. 'I've always believed you. Because I've never known you to tell a lie.'

'Aye, you did as I recall. But that did'ne stop the others making a fool of me.' He reached for his tobacco pouch and prodded some coarse strands into an old pipe.

'Mr Brewer. I am sorry to intrude on you like this, but Annie here has told me something of your wonderful experiences, but I am sure that you can fill in all the details so that I can produce a correct version of what happened.' Kate tried her utmost to be diplomatic, realising that the old man was very touchy and would brook no nonsense.

'Aye well … it's so long ago ye ken, but my memory of that day will never leave me. I don't care what people think.'

Annie and Kate sat back expectantly and Jackie began his diatribe.

'I was living in Glyn Nedd – the Vale of Neath at the time. I had just visited the nearby town and was taking a rest on a roadside rock, my feet were killing me as I remember. There was a waterfall at the back of me; I could hear the thunderous roar as the torrent hit the stones not far from where I sat. Suddenly a pony emerged from the foaming cascade of water and shook the spume from its snow white mane and came toward me.' Jackie shook his head as if to emulate the pony's movement. 'It stood there, dripping wet in the sunlight. Then it whinnied and snorted and tossed its head as if to invite me to mount it. I got up from the rock and walked toward it. It didn't shy away. I was so damn tired that I thought if I could get a ride the rest of the way home, it'd save my legs. He stood still while I clambered on his back from the sloping ground. There was no saddle or bridle but I felt completely safe on his back with my hands in his mane. It was a fine horse. Really fast. In fact the hedges and trees went by so quickly that I thought we were flying. It wouldn't stop. On and on it went, past my house and across the glen. I screamed but could not let go. We galloped on until the evening dusk revealed a full moon matching his white coat.' Jackie's pipe lay unlit in his hand. He shook his head again and turned to the women. 'Ye'll never believe this, but at that moment the horse vanished beneath me and I was thrown to the ground. I lay there a long while not daring to look up or tend to my wounds. It was dawn before I could move and make my way back to my home.'

They sat there in silence absorbing the significance of what Jackie had just told them.

'Ye can either believe me or not. It means nothing to me now. I know it's true. You may have other ideas young lady.' He pointed his remarks to Kate.

'It's a remarkable story. And I do believe that you experienced a weird episode that had a pronounced effect on you. All of us have something that happens at some time or other and find it hard to believe, even ourselves.' Kate thought of what she had been put through – who would believe that? 'Thank you for taking me into your confidence. I am very grateful. I shall follow it up with further experiences if I can find them.'

'I don't think the ones ye'll find end as fortunate as mine. I wish ye luck.'

Annie and Kate said their goodbyes with more thanks. At the door Jackie stopped them and looked them straight in the eye. 'I hear that old Craggy has gone missing. Take care ladies – there may be another Kelpie in the loch. Watch your backs and don't look him in the eye.'

Chapter Twenty Four

It was one of those majestic mornings when the leaves gave of their best in an effort to ward off the ageing process of autumn. A glorious display of greeny-gold mantle on the periphery of larch, oak, and chestnut. Even the loch reflected the rainbow array of colours, never truly matched by artists. The last of the swallows skipped and skimmed the surface of the glassy waters, cowed under the competition from around its shores.

Kate gloried in such days. She had been a keen walker until she married when most of her hobbies had been methodically curtailed. Thinking back she was amazed how little she knew of Angus and his domineering character. But she did now.

Dismissing him from her thoughts, Kate concentrated on keeping a steady pace along the western shore of Loch Garve. Not easy when the path was strewn with pebbles and hubris from the overhanging pines.

In the distance, as she measured how far she ought to venture, she saw a vague shape emerging from the horizon. A shape she had seen before. Gradually growing in size until she recognised the man pounding the soil as Adam. This time all he wore was a brief pair of old jeans cut off at the thigh.

Kate admired the incredible muscular movement of his body, where every part was enhanced by the sheen of his sweat as he pushed himself to the limit.

'Hi,' shouted Kate.

The man stopped short and looked toward her. 'Hello.'

'I'm afraid I couldn't keep that pace, not even on a bicycle,' she laughed.

He grunted, taking a breath and moving nearer to her. 'Walking?' he asked.

'Yes. Thought it about time I caught up on my exercise routine.' She again appraised his body and blushingly said. 'I suppose you keep to a regular programme then?'

'Yes.' His eyes hung deep in his face, brown and sultry. 'Can't let the body waste away.'

'I wouldn't say your body is wasting away.' As soon as she said it, Kate caught her breath and tried to cover the fact that she had been assessing his frame.

'Shall we walk?' he said and Kate found herself automatically turning around and striding along at his side.

He wasn't much of conversationalist, so Kate took the initiative and commented on the surrounding beauty of the loch and the mountains. Eventually she turned to more personal details. 'You haven't live here long have you?'

Adam just nodded.

'Do you like it here?'

'Yes. It's as good as anywhere else.'

Kate plunged in. 'Where were you before you came to Loch Garve.'

There was a silence, then. 'Not too far away.'

'Why did you move then?' Kate hesitated to ask such a pointed question, but it was one she would have put quite ordinarily to anyone else.

He didn't answer. Then he glanced sideways at her and said that he had a job to do.

'Oh.' That stumped her and she did not dare ask what job. Instead she switched tactics and asked about his family. 'Have you relatives in Scotland then?'

'Yes.' Again no explanation.

Kate was getting exasperated and gave up on him. Then he said. 'What brings you to Scotland?'

This was a lot easier and she told him that she was a freelance journalist on a mission for stories for her publishing contacts.

He showed little interest and continued to match her pace which was stretched to match his.

'It's a lonely life up here isn't it?' Kate said innocently. 'I mean, Annie lives alone. You do. There aren't any near neighbours to call for help if you need it and .....'

'You need help?' He stopped surprised.

'Well no. Er .. no, not at the moment. But if we did ..... you know ... we couldn't really stop anyone breaking in, or forcing themselves on us .....'

'Is anyone likely to?' His piercing manner started to show some concern.

'No. Not at the moment.' Kate decided to tell him more of her fears. 'I have been married,' she said.

'Oh. Does that mean you are under threat?'

He doesn't seem to appreciate that all couples who divorce are not under threat. 'I could be. You see, I caught my husband committing a crime and he has just escaped from prison.' Kate stopped and gazed across the loch. 'I think he may want to take revenge. I know it's silly, and I may be looking on the dark side, but it is just a feeling I've got.'

'And you have no weapons in your house?'

'Of course not. Why would two women want guns or anything?'

'You said yourself. You have no means of defending yourselves.' Adam's logic was getting to Kate and she turned and walked on. Adam followed. 'If what you say is true, you need to get some sort of defence in case your ex-husband does come looking for you.'

'What would you suggest? We haven't even got a telephone.'

Adam came back with the obvious. 'Then get one.' He took Kate by the arm and she was shaken by the tremor that shot through her. At that moment she knew she couldn't do anything about it if he took her in her arms. Did she want him to? Why was she trembling beneath the warm plaid jacket?

'I suppose we could have a telephone put in. That would give us more immediate contact with others.' Kate's forehead furrowed. 'Do you have one?'

'No. But I could have one and then I would be available if you needed me.' Adam's statement was factual and said with no intent to promote himself as a guardian angel.

'What about the other? You know … the weapon.' Kate couldn't bring herself to say "gun."

'I could get you one. You'll need a licence, but that is easy in these parts.'

They came to the path which led up to the main road near to Annie's cottage. Kate held out her hand and Adam took it in his, holding it for a fraction longer than Kate anticipated, but nevertheless enjoyed every tingling second. 'Bye,' she said. 'I'll come to see you about the arrangements if that is OK?'

Kate could swear that his previous impassive face softened for a moment as he replied. 'Yes. That would be good.'

She watched as he sprinted off on bare feet, the perfectly shaped V of his back ingraining itself on her memory and once again inviting a shiver of excitement she had never experienced since her schooldays and her first kiss.

Chapter Twenty Five

With the new telephone duly installed, Kate was eager to contact the outside world. Although she enjoyed the solitude and peace of a slower environment, she felt an itching to talk to someone familiar. Detective Inspector Clare Baddeley was her first choice.

The Inspector had always been a supporter of Kate through all of her troubles and her compassion for the mess that was now her life. This had had a big impact on her. Now was the time to be brought up to date about any news of Angus and how the search was proceeding.

After three rings Kate was put through to Inspector Baddeley by the duty officer.

'Hi Kate, how are you doing?' The everyday relaxed voice of the inspector seemed to reassure Kate more than she realised she needed to be.

'I'm fine. Enjoying the space and relaxation.' Kate laughed nervously. 'Good to get away from the treadmill for a time.'

'I'm pleased to hear it. Take your time. You know when you will be ready to take up the reins again.' The inspector paused. 'Is there anything particular you rang me for?'

'Yes. I heard about the escape.' Kate was lost for a way to enquire how matters were at that end. 'I … er .. wondered if there has been any definite news. Any sort of trace of where he might have gone.'

There was a hesitation a shade too long in the reply. 'We are doing everything we possibly can.' Inspector Baddeley laughed. 'God, that sounds like an announcement to the press doesn't it?' She continued. 'However, I will be frank with you. We haven't established much in our search. We have traced a car he bought after the escape, but by now, that will have been swapped for another. We have no indication of where he is heading. He tried to throw us a googly, by setting up a false trail south, but that's as far as we got. Being an ex copper, he knows how we operate and I am trying to figure out what his intentions are.'

'Has he been to our old house?'

'Not as far as we are aware. We searched naturally, but everything appeared to be in order. But.' She took a deep breath. 'If, as I suspect he is going north, then he would have wanted some sort of basic requirements. Other clothes, money, etc. He could either get these at the house, which he hasn't, or another of his secret store places. Rental firms and estate agents are all being questioned for the names of their lessees and all bank accounts that we know of, checked. He cannot gain access to your account as it is now in your sole name. Do you know of any other accounts he may have had?'

'No. But then he wouldn't have told me would he?' Kate said resignedly. 'He always had plenty of cash available. More than you would expect a working copper to have. It never occurred to me that he was involved in that side of crime, until … well you know – he was caught for the other.' It still pained Kate to refer to her ex-husband's propensity for young females. It made her feel dirty.

'I know Kate. And that is one thing that we are keeping our eyes open for. As a matter of fact, there have been reports of two young girls missing in Kiltarlity and Marybank. One twelve the other thirteen. These happened soon after his escape. Could be a co-incidence, but we can't take that chance. The Scottish constabulary are following up on both.'

In her mind's eye Kate traced a map from Manchester to Scotland. Both towns were unknown to her.

'Hold on a moment while I get a map.' Annie always kept one under the telephone table. She noted that both towns were on a direct route between Loch Ness and Loch Garve.

'He's coming after me isn't he?' Kate's quiet voice was emphatic and in a tone of resignation. 'The bastard's on his way, but can't resist his penchant for young girls to feed his sick mind.'

'We don't know that Kate. We don't even know if he has gone north. There has been no sight of him or trace of the vehicle bought in Lymm. He knows how to disappear, how to exist without contact with the world around him.' Inspector Baddeley was sympathetic to Kate's fears, but had to maintain the routine of logical investigation before jumping to any conclusion. 'I am trying to think like him as difficult as it seems, but we have a good knowledge of his character now, but he has a devious personality and is well versed in police detection methods. He will do the exact opposite of what we expect of him. That could be his undoing. We also are concentrating on unlikely alternatives to our usual channels of detection.'

'Has anyone at the station given any clue as to where I am?' Again Kate posed the question in an investigative manner. 'The only way he could find me, is by way of the police. I did not tell anyone where I intended to go. Only you and your superiors know that I am in Scotland. There has been no correspondence, no contact since I left, but you know how rumours circulate, someone could have made an educated guess, given that I have talked about my friend from time to time.'

'Good point Kate. I will question all the staff, especially the telephone officers for any strange calls which may concern you. These would only have been made recently so it is a good chance that something will turn up. In the meantime, there is no need to feel apprehensive. The escape has been circulated nationally and all forces will be on the lookout for him. He will surface sometime and then we shall have a definite lead.'

'I know I am on extended leave, but as I know my ex-husband better than most, I am asking permission to investigate from up here. At the moment I am posing as a freelance writer and that allows me to access people for questioning....'

'Now wait a moment Kate ...'

'No. Whatever is relevant will be relayed to you and I will not interfere in the official investigation.' Kate took a breath. 'Remember I was instrumental in catching him first time. He won't expect me to be hunting him.' She laughed. 'The hunter being hunted.'

'Not as I would want it, but I don't suppose I can stop you from asking questions of people. But be careful. He is more dangerous now than he ever was. He has murdered and will do again if provoked. Do you have a gun?'

Inspector Baddeley's last question shook Kate. She had never been involved in firearms in the police and the thought brought back Adam's advice to protect themselves. 'No, but that has been put to me by a friend of mine. I never realised that it would become a necessity so soon.'

'I am not advocating that you should shoot him on sight, but a disturbing factor arose when we questioned all MacManus's colleagues as to any significant indication of him being a "bad 'un." One fact emerged. The armed response team were short of one Walther issue handgun from a raid after one of them was injured.' Kate held her breath. 'It was never traced and MacManus was the last to leave the scene.'

Katc heaved a silent gasp. 'He's well prepared isn't he? Free and no doubt expertly covering his tracks, he could be anywhere. But I will bet my pension that he is on his way here. After me.'

Chapter Twenty Six

Annie came in from her morning's work gathering bric-a-brac for her stall.

'Whatever's the matter Kate? You look as if you've seen a ghost.' She took her in her arms and gave her a hug. 'What you need is a good stiff drink. And I'll have one too,' she laughed.

Annie's humour broke the tension in Kate and she joined her friend in a single malt that certainly put things into perspective.

'He's coming up here Annie. He is leaving his trademark deliberately to frighten me,' Kate explained her conversation with Inspector Baddeley. 'I think I'll take Adam's advice and get that gun. We might need it.'

'Do you really think that he will go as far as that?' said an incredulous Annie.

'You don't know him like I do.'

'But he doesn't know you're here. And he certainly doesn't know your new name. How can he find you?'

Kate nodded slowly. 'Oh, he will. He's good at tracking people. I'll give him that.' She rose and put on her coat. 'I'll go and see Adam now. We need some sort of protection in case Angus comes calling.'

'I'll come with you.'

'No Annie. This is my problem. Let me sort it. I don't want to put you in any danger.' She pulled her woolly hat over her forehead and strode down the path to the road, every inch a woman on a mission.

Annie watched her go and shook her head. Whatever happened, she would stand by Kate against any threat from whatever source.

The telephone rang. Surprised, Annie picked it up. 'Yes?'

'Annie?' said the voice. 'Is that you?'

Annie took a deep breath. 'What the hell are you doing on my telephone?'

'Just wanted to speak to you. I miss your voice.'

'You should have thought about that a long time ago. What gives you the right to contact me again? I thought that was all settled when we broke up.'

'Ohh Annie, that was all a mistake. I don't know what happened, but I can see now that I was wrong to run out on you like that.'

'Listen Andy,' Annie could hardly bear to say his name. 'We are finished. Caput. Done with. Got it? Never ring me again. I never want anything to do with you now, in the future, or forever. Get lost!'

Annie slammed the telephone down and held her head in her hands. Who the hell did he think he was ringing her like that? And why was he contacting her now? Broke up with his piece of skirt I'll bet, she guessed. Well bully for her. Seen some sense at last.

She tried to dismiss him from her mind, but the voice remained in her head. What is it with these husbands? Think they're God almighty? She resolved that if he rang again to slam the phone down immediately.

I need another pick me up she convinced herself as she made her way into the kitchen. Drinking at this time of day – does that constitute alcoholism? So what if it did. I enjoy it and if I'm the only one who is harmed, then the world can take a hop, skip and a jump.

I wonder how Kate is getting on with Adam? The thought struck her for no reason at all, except she had noted a certain appreciation of Adam's talents from her bosom friend. Not that she didn't fancy him as well, but that was only her way of weighing up all likely contenders for her charms. Not that there are that many she could choose. She laughed at her daydreams, but still wondered if Kate was really taken with the hunk that lived just up the road. She would see.

She picked up the telephone directory that had accompanied the installation of the telephone and looked under "McBride." Yes, there it was for all to see. She hadn't thought of that. Then she had another thought. Suppose Angus had the same idea. He knew her married name and it would take him about two seconds to connect the name to Kate. Oh my God, what have we done? Hastily she looked at the page again. There were only seven McBride's listed. Wouldn't take a genius to figure out which one was Annie McBride.

'I hope Kate brings back that bloody gun,' she swore. And soon.

Chapter Twenty Seven

There is much searching to do. It is as we expected. He has gone on to other lochs and may be operating from these. He is aware of our mission and is trying to avoid any contact in his usual haunts. Follow him and try and force him to return to Loch Garve. That is where you will eventually be able to carry out your duty.

Do we know where he has gone?

Only south. There are many lochs to choose from. The most likely are the lochs above Loch Ness. They will suit his purpose. But he will be out of his normal surroundings and not familiar with the environment. He may be too wary to go on the land until he has adjusted to the territory. But you must find him. He will take what is on offer and must be prevented at all costs. It may be that it is too late. But persevere in your search.

I will go tomorrow and make enquiries. The usual superstitions will be raised, but if there is any evidence that rings true then I will find him.

Good. Maintain your connection with the two women. You may need them when the time comes.

Chapter Twenty Eight

'It's time we got to the bottom of all this,' said Kate. 'I've heard so many varying version of this wraith or whatever it is, that I am getting confused.' She turned to Annie. 'Is there a good library within driving distance?'

'Yes. I believe there is one at Dingwall. Why?' Annie's brow furrowed as to why Kate required a library.

'We may be able to get a definitive description of this wraith and an expert explanation of the myth.'

'I thought you didn't believe in it,' said Annie, smiling behind her drink.

'I don't. But that doesn't stop me researching it to confirm whatever opinion I have.' Kate looked triumphantly at Annie. 'Anyway, we could do with a good day out.'

'True. You've been through a lot lately and a change of scenery will do us both good.'

They made for the kitchen to make a few sandwiches, not forgetting a bottle of decent wine, grabbed their coats and jumped into Annie's van.

The sun shone and for once there was no sign of rain. 'Once we've visited the library and discovered whatever you want to discover, we can picnic by Loch Achonachie, it's on our way back anyway.' Annie explained that it was a short distance from the town and was immediately south of Loch Garve.

'Good idea. It will give us the right atmosphere to discuss what we find.' Then with a wicked chuckle Kate said. 'Who knows? We might even be visited by one of these wraiths after our food.'

Annie laughed and was glad that Kate was relaxing again after her initial worry about Angus.

The trip was uneventful and they entered the public library shortly before lunch.

An old Victorian building, but packed with rooms on all subjects. Kate was looking for the non-fiction section and a helpful assistant pointed the way.

'Here it is,' said Annie. 'You'll find what you're looking for in here.'

'Have you never been here before Annie?' asked Kate.

'No. Never had much time for books after school, and even then I didn't particularly enjoy reading them.'

'You don't know what you're missing. Losing yourself in a good yarn is the best exercise I know.'

'Speaking of yarns, this section here might interest you.' Annie read. '"Myths and legends of Scotland."'

Kate looked along the row of books and suddenly stopped dead. 'Look at this!' she said. Annie came over and read the title. '"The Kelpie of Loch Garve."'

'Well I never,' said Annie. So all those tales have a basis which someone has taken the trouble to write about.'

Kate took the book from the shelf and read the opening paragraph. '"The Kelpie is a water horse said to lure humans, especially children, into the water to drown and eat them." Ugh, that doesn't seem too promising.' She went on quoting. '"It performs this act by encouraging children to ride on its back. Once its victims fall into the trap, the Kelpie's skin becomes adhesive and it takes them into the water, dragging them to the bottom and devouring them."'

'That's impossible,' exclaimed Annie. 'I've never heard such nonsense. Just a bunch of tittle-tattle garnered from over imaginative individuals and presented as fact.'

'What about old Jackie's tale then? He didn't want to broadcast it and doesn't care if anyone believes him or not. I grant you that it sounds incredible, but there is a touch of reality to it.' Kate was thinking of the night she saw the man and then the horse and both disappearing into the loch. Or did they?

'Let's take this book and study it over lunch. It may give us a much more considered opinion without the far-fetched stories no doubt highly coloured accounts by impressionable people. The fact remains that the description of the wraith is consistent in nearly all of the definitions. It is only the related experiences that tend to lend an air of disbelief to the myth.'

Annie shook her head. 'I wish you wouldn't get involved in this. No good will come of it, mark my words.'

Kate laughed and tucked the book under her arm and raced Annie to the van. 'Bet you can't outrun me, let alone a Kelpie!'

'Don't joke about it. You're putting the wind up me.'

'No more than running to the van will do,' taunted Kate as she easily beat her companion, having had more physical training than Annie over the past fourteen years or so.

The picnic was all the more enjoyable because of the unusually hot, sunny afternoon. The wine helped to put a dreamy quality on the flora surrounding them, with rustling of leaves continually being picked up and discarded by the intermittent breeze.

'Perfect,' said Annie.

'Agree,' said Kate. 'Who said life's dull when you get off the fast lane?'

'Come and try it, say I. I never realised until I moved to my cottage that a slowing down was all I needed to create a happiness that I hadn't dreamed of.' She finished her last glass of wine and lay back on the car rug. 'Wake me when it's time for bed.'

Kate stayed in a sitting position, studying her book. There was a great amount of detail about the various "Kelpies" and their counterparts in other parts of the world. Some good, some bad. One particular talent of the water horse was to turn itself into human form. Probably another one of the more embroidered accounts of some deluded person trying to get out of a predicament.

One far fetched legend was where a water horse had been chastised by his wife to get a proper fireplace. Kate gasped at the incredulous idea. Apparently the water horse had gone ashore from the depths and found a builder, transported him to his home and told him to build a magnificent fireplace with a chimney and if he did, the builder would never want for fish again. People swore thereafter that the builder had more than enough fish for the remainder of his life. Moreover, it was said that on cold winter nights, a certain trace of smoke issued from precisely where the builder had told everyone that he had built the fireplace.

Believe that one if you can, smiled Kate. Load of old codswallop, as my mother used to say.

Mind you, she had a few "tall tales" of her own.

Tired after her lunch, Kate leaned back on her elbows and surveyed the scene before her. What was the name of this loch again? Annie had said Loch Achonochie hadn't she? With a name like that you would hardly forget it. Where was the nearest town apart from Dingwall?

Kate went to the van and dug out Annie's road map. Scruffy and handled by years of oil engrained fingers, she found the page she was looking for. She quickly looked up Marybank. As she suspected it was quite close to Loch Achonachie where they now were. Quickly locating the other town Inspector Baddeley had mentioned – Kiltarlity, she almost lost her breath. That too was near to Loch Bruicheach. Two towns; two disappearances of young girls;

two lochs nearby. Was that too much of a co-incidence? Was her theory that Angus might have been responsible for the two girls missing; wrong?

This is where she would start her investigation, she decided. Both sets of parents could give her the information that she needed.

It would confirm either that Angus was in the area or that the mythical claims of several eyewitnesses would be lent more weight to their authenticity.

Whichever came up following her enquiries, it didn't solve the problem of where the children were. Deep down in the depths, or deep down in some lonely grave.

Kate prayed that the children had just run away and that they would be found before either of the possibilities came into the frame.

Chapter Twenty Nine

Angus MacManus watched from a safe distance as the school gates opened and the chattering, excited children surged out like water out of a spout. Running here and there, they were gathered up by overprotective parents and whisked away for a school-free weekend.

He carefully noted which ones were collected and which ones weren't. The latter he guessed had houses quite near the school and it was thought unnecessary for them to be escorted home.

Four or five took his eye. One especially well developed youngster, not long out of primary school, strode along the path, oblivious to the shouts of her companions to "come and have a play in the fields."

A loner.

Worldly wise? He doubted it. You only picked that up from your association with other school friends. Tall for her age, with a springy gait that would someday develop into the sort of walk that attracted all sorts of men. Would she ever get to that stage? smiled Angus.

He started his camper van and cruised by the girl, stopping about a hundred yards farther on, just past a road junction. If she carried straight on he knew she lived in the nearby development. If she turned left, there were just six houses in the cul-de-sac.

She turned left.

He reversed into the cul-de-sac as if to change direction, but it gave him a rear mirror view of which house she entered. The first on the right.

He drove off the way he had come and found a parking place some distance past the school. Opposite the car park, he was faced with a slight incline before the dramatic escarpment of a towering cliff blotted out the lower part of the sky. The greenery ran along the back of the school and continued toward the estate further up the road. In between was the cul-de-sac.

Walking at a brisk pace he traversed the school building below and made his way to the back of where the child lived. A perfect view of the house, both front door and back.

He settled down to wait.

Within an hour the back door opened and a girl emerged, changed out of her uniform into suitable clothes for outdoors. She looked neither left nor right as she swung her legs purposefully down to the main road. At the bottom she turned right towards where Angus had left his van.

He made a quicker pace on the way back and was in time to stand by his van before the girl came into sight.

'I wonder if you could help me?' Angus said.

The girl looked curiously at him but did not reply.

'I'm looking for a chap called McBride. It struck me that possibly he may have a child at your school and I could find him through her.'

'No,' the girl shook her head. 'There's no-one of that name in my class, and as far as I know, not in the school either.'

'Oh, how disappointing.' He slid open the side door. 'Look – this is the district where I was told I might find him.' He pulled out a map onto the seat and indicated that she should have a look. 'This is the right area isn't it?'

The girl stepped forward and peered at the map.

From his pocket Angus took the swab soaked in chloroform and clamped it around the girl's mouth. There was a muffled gasp, a slight struggle, then nothing. It was simple to heave the body over the seat and into the main body of the camper van. The curtains had been drawn and within two minutes the whole operation was complete and Angus was driving off congratulating himself on his expertise.

No, he said to himself, you won't be swinging those hips for anyone else to enjoy.

Chapter Thirty

'Let's invite Adam to tea.' Kate's statement came right out of the blue.

'Whatever has given you that idea?' queried Annie.

'Oh, just that it seems a rather neighbourly thing to do, that's all.' Kate was defensive.

'Is that all it is about?'

'Well no. I want to probe him some more about his background, his family, where her comes from. We've never found anything out about him have we?'

Annie smiled. 'And are you sure that's all this invitation is about?'

'Yes. Why?' Kate looked Annie straight in the eye and giggled. 'Well, there is another reason. He is rather a dashing fellow isn't he? And I'm getting bored with looking at female company every mealtime.'

'You're quite right. It is time we showed some community spirit. Apart from that I could do with some male company. Not a lot of it about at the moment.'

'I'm sorry that Andy took it in his head to phone you. It must have been a shock. I mean no warning or anything.' Kate fully understood the feeling. How would she react if Angus took it in his head to phone her?

'Forget about it. It was something and nothing. Feeling sorry for himself I suppose. Well I don't,' Annie said defensively. 'Let him find some other bimbo to pour his heart out to.'

'So when shall we invite him then?'

'Who? … oh, Adam you mean. This Sunday would be a good time. All day free from any chores. How about tea time-ish? Start with hors d'oeuvres and then carry on from there. I might even have a bit of venison in the freezer. Saving it for something like this.' Annie skipped into the kitchen to check on her stores.

Kate started to make a list of the points she wanted to cover with Adam without it looking as though she was prying. But she was wasn't she? she admitted.

'I didn't tell you did I that when we were on that picnic the other day, I discovered that the two missing children came from near the two nearby lochs. Bit creepy eh?' Kate shouted to Annie in the kitchen.

'Why? Do you think that the Kelpie got them then?' Annie gave a cynical laugh. 'But you don't believe in them do you?'

'No. But then I don't believe in angels, but there must be some I'm sure. Perhaps Adam can give us his opinion.'

Again Annie looked quizzically at Kate. 'You really have got that man on your mind haven't you? Are you falling for him?'

'Course not! I hardly know him.' Kate tried to sound convincing but didn't.

'I didn't know Andy but I fell for him. More fool me.' Annie ruefully knocked her fist against her head. 'I'll know better next time.'

'Is there going to be a next time?'

'Probably not. Love them and leave them, that's my motto from now on.'

Kate pointed her finger. 'Not with Adam though. He's too nice a chap to mess about with.'

'I'd like to mess about with him all the same, wouldn't you?' Annie dug Kate in the ribs and busied herself with writing down a menu for Sunday.

'Whose going round to invite him then?'

'You are of course,' replied Annie. 'I think he has taken a shine to you also.'

'Don't be silly. I've only talked to him two or three times. He's very shy. No … that's not right. He is very withdrawn, that's a better word. Doesn't say a lot if he doesn't have to. So remember, don't dominate the conversation, try to let him do the talking.'

'Yes ma'am. As you say ma'am. He's all yours. Only if there's a little bit left over, think of me won't you. I could do with a bit of resurrection of my libido. It's had no attention lately.'

Kate laughed at her friend. Neither have I, she thought. Does this lonely life get any better? she wondered. Or was a man essential to satisfy the inner needs? Does the yearning go away? Or does it mellow and fade into fond memories? I hope not, she muttered under her breath.

'I'll just go along and test the water with Adam then. No time like the present.'

'OK,' said Annie. 'Oh; ask him if he has any spinach. Go nicely with the venison. Put a bit of get up and go in you as well.'

Annie's last remark reminded Kate that her get up and go had been neglected and she was determined to wake it up again. A nice run along the loch shore would be ideal for getting her fitness up to the mark. She ignored the fact that it might coincide with Adam's daily run.

Chapter Thirty One

Kate started her undercover investigation the next day. She borrowed Annie's van after dropping her off at the market stall in Strathpeffer.

A half hour later and she drove into the first of the two towns where the lost girls lived. Marybank on the A 832. Not very big but the usual amenities of a post office, pub and general store. She looked up the address she had been given by Inspector Baddeley and found the avenue quite easily.

A council estate of about a hundred houses, all designed and situated like some child's playbox. The paint was either green or brown. The tenants probably had no choice over the colour, but with the cheap rents there was no complaint.

Kate knocked at the rather weather beaten door. A jerk from the other side at last managed to free the door from its swollen frame. A plump, florid face peered at Kate over a dirty apron. 'What do you want?' The voice was as gruff as the soiled apron.

'I wonder if I could have a word with you about Lesley. I'm not from the police,' Kate quickly assured the woman. 'I am working for a national publication and wish to put your side of the story to the readers. The police often overlook this and I've always found that it reaches a far wider readership than official releases to the press.'

The woman stood there trying to decipher the explanation that Kate had given. She shook her head and said. 'The police have already taken my statement. What more can I tell you.' She thought a while. 'And why should I?'

'It may help to trace her last movements. Someone may have seen her on that day. Or noticed something suspicious.' Before the woman could object Kate hurried on. 'They may have even seen her hitching a lift or something to indicate that she was running away.'

'She'd never run away from here. What are you implying?' The woman, who Kate assumed was the mother began to turn nasty.

'No. I'm not saying that.' Kate smiled. 'Can we continue this conversation inside please? We don't want the neighbours nosing do we?' Kate knew she had hit a chord when the woman looked at the houses opposite and saw curtains moving.

'Nosy bastards. Can't do anything in private around here.' She stepped back and Kate entered.

There was a small porch with just enough room for the both of them. Through an adjoining door was the living room. Couldn't call it a lounge, thought Kate, there is only one armchair and a battered settee. A table stuck up the corner and Victorian sideboard completed the furnishing.

Hesitant to sit in the armchair, Kate leant against the table.

'What do you want to know then?' The woman's sharp voice ground against the eardrums as Kate explained that it had never been established exactly where Lesley had been seen last.

'School, then here,' the woman answered.

'Surely someone, other children must have seen her outside the gates? She wouldn't have left on her own would she?'

'No .. I suppose not. There were that girl friend of hers. She always hangs about with her at playtime. I've seen them when I passed.'

'What is her name?' Kate had her pad out now and tried to look like a reporter.

'Claire, I think. Yes Claire Brown. I remember that now because of our name "Green." Colours you see. Go together. Not like the rest of them with posh names ….'

'Where does she live, this Claire?'

'Not far from here. Top of the street. Last house. They look down on us, because we live at the bottom. Claire's all right though. Skinny with long pigtails. Like a jack rabbit.' The woman pulled out a cigarette. She didn't offer Kate one.

'And was Lesley OK when she went to school that day? No tantrums. No indication that she was worried or anything like that?' Kate hastily rushed to assure the woman that she wasn't implying that Lesley had been any of these things.

'She were all right. Moody as usual. Didn't like school much but she knew what she'd get if she didn't go.' Kate looked at the woman's hefty arms poking out of the rather soiled blouse that she wore. Instant punishment came to mind.

'Was she in uniform?' Kate knew that Angus had a fetish for uniforms, he had tried it once with her.

'Course she was. As good as anybody else's. Took a pride in that she did. Cost a packet too.' She failed to mention that it had been subsidised by the local council because of their poor circumstances.

'Did Lesley have any particular hobbies or pastimes? Sports and things like that?'

'She liked walking. Spent hours wandering all over the place. I told her not to go near that loch. Too deep and dangerous. Never know what's lurking around there.' She stared at Kate as if challenging her to contradict her.

Kate noted this down and asked. 'What do you think has happened to her Mrs Green?'

'Dunno. Nobody tells me nothing.' She almost shed a tear. 'I just miss her that's all.'

Despite all the squalor, there was a genuine feeling of loss of someone close to the woman. Kate felt compassion for her and realised that whatever the conditions of a home, there is still the human factor of love somewhere between people.

'Thank you for your time Mrs Green. You have been a great help. Let's hope that Lesley comes home soon.' Kate touched Mrs Green's arm with a warm smile as she made for the door.

'You'll tell me if you find out anything won't you?'

The woman's last plea was heartbreaking.

'You'll be the first Mrs Green. I promise.'

Let's hope it isn't the outcome that is now almost inevitable. The first four days are days of hope. After that the chances of discovery are practically nil.

An uncomfortable feeling of doom hung around her as she made her way to the neighbour's house at the top of the street.

A dead copy of the previous house with the exception that there was a well kept lawn with flower beds and a newly painted front door. Decent curtains were visible through the window and the reception equally as presentable. 'Yes?'

'I have called about the missing child. I understand that your daughter and she were pals.'

'Yes they were. Although goodness knows why. They were completely different in temperament and well … you know … she is not from what you could call a decent family background.'

'Yes.' Kate decided not to go into that avenue and asked if she could come in for a moment.

'Of course.'

Kate stepped over the threshold and noted the clean carpets and tidy front room. Flowers were on the table and good smell of roast chicken was coming from the kitchen. 'I'm sorry if I have caught you at an awkward moment, but I am keen to establish exactly when Lesley Green was last seen.' Kate went on to tell the lady that she was an investigate reporter for a magazine and wanted to bring a wider readership into being aware of the disappearance. 'The national magazines very rarely get involved with anything this side of the border.'

'Of course. Would you like a word with my daughter?'

'If that's possible – yes. Thank you.' Kate waited expectantly for the daughter to be called downstairs.

'Hello Claire.' The girl was everything that Mrs Green had described. Skinny, with a sharp face and pigtails. 'I'm a freelance writer and would like you to tell me about the last time you saw Lesley. I know you have been through all this with the police, but I may be able to put a different slant on it and hopefully pinpoint more accurately where she may have gone, or what might have happened to her.'

Claire looked at her mum for support. Mrs Brown nodded.

'We left school at the usual time of 4.15pm and played about a bit in the playground. Some boys were teasing us and we skirted around them and made for the front gate. There were some parents waiting, although not many. My mum let's me come home by myself.'

Kate smiled at Mrs Brown and nodded her approval.

'When we got to the gate, instead of turning left with me as usual, Lesley stopped and said she was going for a walk. "Down by the loch," I think she said.

'You're sure she said "by the loch?"' said Kate.

'Yes. I thought it odd, but then I remembered that she had done this before when she wanted to think.'

'How do you know that she wanted to think? Did she say anything else apart from what you've just told me?'

Claire pulled her pigtail across her mouth. 'No. That was it. "I want to think before I go home" she said.'

'Was she worried about anything?'

'She was always worrying about things at home. She said that her dad wasn't very nice to her mother, and that her mother could improve herself if she wanted. Things like that.' Again the pigtail was in her mouth as if to mask what she was saying. Claire seemed embarrassed to be talking of her friend like that.

'Did you watch her walk away?'

'Yes. As far as the pathway that led down to the loch. Then I turned and came home.'

'What time would that be then? Half past four?' Claire nodded.

'Did you notice anything different in the days before. Any strange cars, men, anything that was not usual?' Kate noticed Claire hesitate before answering.

'Not particularly. There was always a crush of us trying to get out first and I didn't particularly look around for strangers or anything.' She shrugged her shoulders. 'Although -'

'Yes?'

' – once I thought I saw a sort of vehicle that I hadn't seen before. A large van – with windows. And curtains. And one of those roofs that lifts up. I've seen them by the loch when people come to stay overnight.'

'A camper van. The sort you sleep in. Is that it?'

'Yes.'

'Where was it when you saw it?' Kate kept her excitement under control as best she could.

'Some way from the school. I passed it on my way home.'

'Do you remember the colour?'

'I think it was blue .... but could have been white.'

'Was there anybody in it?' Kate held her breath.

'No. It looked empty.' She looked at her mum again. 'I'm sorry.'

'Nothing to be sorry for Claire. You've done very well. Thank you.' Kate gave the girl a re-assuring smile and stood.

'Thank you Mrs Brown. That's the nearest I think we'll get to the disappearance. 'Oh, just one thing more Claire. Do any of the children turn right out of the gates – like Lesley did?'

Claire thought. 'Only one. The rest of us live mostly on this estate or further towards the town.'

'What is this other girl's name?'

'Shirley. Shirley Conroy. She lives about a quarter mile on the same road as the school. Big old house.'

Kate thanked Claire and her mum once again and made for Annie's van.

The dreaded picture being created in her mind was taking hold of her stomach. The classical stalker routine as old as the hills, but one which countless young girls never seemed to comprehend until it was too late.

The same routine used by her ex-husband Angus MacManus.

Chapter Thirty Two

'Are you sure he said that he would come?' Annie was anxiously looking out of the front window.

'Of course I'm sure. I told him to come around five o'clock like you said.'

'Well he's late!' Annie rushed into the kitchen again to attend to her meat.

'He's not late. It's only a couple of minutes before five.' Kate too peered around the curtains for signs of Adam. He would be walking and she tried to see over the hedge at the side of the cottage.

'And what did you do all that time you were at his house?' The call came from the kitchen in between oven doors slamming and pots being moved on the hob.

'I wasn't that long,' protested Kate. 'I was looking at his garden.

'Yes. And what was he looking at?'

Kate burst into laughter. 'Not me that's for sure. I was in my working clothes remember? Scruffy jeans and a sweater.'

'Perhaps he likes the country type. You know – willing to get their hands dirty.' Annie came into the room with a beam in her eye. 'You don't have to tell me that you're taken with him. I can see it every time we meet him.'

'Have you seen your own expression when he's around?' retorted Kate. 'You almost devour him with your behaviour.'

'I do not! Anyway there's no harm in looking is there?' Annie primped her hair and looked at her makeup in the mirror. 'Have I overdone it then?'

'You'll do. But I think I'll just pop upstairs to change this blouse. I've noticed a small snag on the sleeve.'

'And put one on that doesn't look like you are trying to be like Jane Russell.' Annie's shout echoed up the stairs as Kate looked down at her décolletage and decided that perhaps it was a trifle over the top.

Not that she thought that Adam had any of those sort of feelings or would be embarrassed by a woman's body.

When she had visited him to invite him to dinner, he had shown a respectful response but had not indicated like any other red blooded man, that he looked forward to being charmed by two females.

On their walk around his smallholding, he had pointed out all the good features of his crops, the multiple salad plants and various vegetables, all healthy and sturdy in the dark earth. But his pride was reserved for his two strong horses. Short but sturdy, with coats as black as jet and smooth as sealskin. But their eyes fascinated Kate. Large pools of unfathomable darkness, surrounded by a thin white line emphasising the deepness of the ebony tint.

They had looked at Kate without moving. Appearing to absorb the very emotion in her body. She had never seen any animals as beautiful as these. And she told Adam as they walked back to the house.

'They are very precious to me,' was all he said.

'Adam, if you don't mind me asking,' said Kate. 'Where do you originate from?' She saw him hesitate. 'I mean where were you before you came to live here?'

After a few strides he said. 'Further north. Well into the highlands.'

'Did you live alone?'

Adam turned to face Kate. 'Sometimes.'

Kate could see that she wasn't going to get any further with that line of questioning. 'You must excuse me. I'm being very rude, but it's my normal way of getting stories for my magazines. Inquisitive that's all.'

'No problem,' Adam turned to look at her. 'If I may ask. Where do you come from?"

Kate smiled. Now the boot was on the other foot. 'From Manchester. I am here for a rest cure, if that's what you call it. I am afraid that my nerves were a little shaken by an experience I had. I thought the peace and quiet would do me good.'

'And has it?'

'Yes. I think it has.' Kate reflected. It really has released a lot of tension but she was more exhilarated by the fact that she was back in her normal detective routine again. She was surprised that it had given her such a boost when she had visited the two girls.

'And when do you intend to return to Manchester?' They had reached the back door and Adam opened it for her.

'Oh, when I'm ready,' said Kate nonchalantly.

'It is a good life here. The soil is good. The air is fresh. And the surroundings are not matched anywhere else.' His simple statement matched his manner. Serene and impregnable.

Kate knew that Annie and she would have a job delving into this closed shop that stood before her.

'So you will come then?' Kate reminded him of the purpose of her visit.

'Of course. I cannot refuse such a generous offer.' For one moment Kate thought that she detected a slightly cynical smile touch his lips. Then it was gone. She continued to look at those lips for longer than was polite, but Adam didn't appear to notice.

'About five o'clock then,' she shouted as she skipped down the path. Why she skipped she wouldn't admit to herself, but she felt good.

'Hurry up. He's here!' Kate heard the shout as she was coming down the stairs. She stopped to look out of the landing window. Adam was dressed casually. Jeans and an open necked check shirt that sat on his perfectly developed shoulders. Just like the advertisements in the women's weekly magazines, she mused.

Adam stood in the doorway admiring the sitting room. 'This is charming,' he said. 'The colours match your personality. Lively and bright, with a professional colour match. I like it.'

Annie was dumfounded. No one had ever commented on her décor. Except Kate when she first arrived. 'Thank you.' She noticed that his expression hadn't change to boost his remarks. Still unfathomable.

'Would you like a drink Adam? Wine, whisky, soft drink?' Kate's hand indicated the sideboard where an array of bottles stood.

'Water please.'

Kate hesitated and then went into the kitchen. 'I hope you don't mind tap water, that's all there is.'

'Finest drink in the world. Pure and nearly unadulterated. Whatever chemicals are being put in should be withdrawn. No one ever caught anything before they introduced "refinements."'

'True. I've chilled it for you,' said Kate as she came through the door.

Adam took the water and took a long draught. 'Good,' he said. 'Top it up please.'

'I'll bring you a large ewer and you can help yourself.' Kate went back to the kitchen.

'So how are you liking it around here?' Annie started off the conversation as she sat in one of the easy chairs. Adam sat himself in the corner of the sofa.

'Fine. There is plenty to do, plenty to see. Lots of places to visit.' He looked directly at Annie. 'I suppose you know this area very well.'

'Well, yes. I get around quite a bit with my job.'

'I noticed that your van wasn't parked outside the other day.'

Annie nodded. 'We went on a picnic. Kate wanted to do some research for her piece in the magazine. We stayed in a lovely field overlooking Loch Achonachie. Do you know it?'

'Does he know what?' asked Kate as she brought the ewer for Adam.

'We were discussing our trip to the other lochs two days ago. I was asking Adam if he knew them. What was the name of the second loch Kate?' Annie took a sip of her white wine and sat back with a twinkle in her eye. Kate sat on the opposite end of the sofa to Adam.

'Loch Achonachie was one and the other is called Loch Bruicheach. You know very well Annie.' Kate saw the mischievous look in her friend's face and giggled. 'You just wanted to hear me pronounce the names didn't you?' She blushed at Adam. 'Annie doesn't think that I can follow the Scottish accent all that well.'

Adam smiled, Kate was pleased to note. 'I have noticed.' He joined in the general cheery banter. 'I have visited both lochs recently and they are beautiful.'

In the kitchen Kate whispered to Annie that she thought that they had broken the ice with Adam. The first signs that he was not the dour, but polite and silent type had begun to emerge.

Over an excellent dinner of venison cooked to perfection with all the roast trimmings and apple pie and custard to follow, Annie and Kate gradually encouraged Adam to talk about himself. The fact that both had consumed several glasses of wine, whilst Adam had stuck to water, helped them to keep up the jollity. Adam seemed to enjoy it.

'So where were you born Adam?' Annie blurted out. 'Sorry. Didn't mean to pry, but I don't understand why you have no broad Scots accent.'

'You weren't born around these parts you tell me, but you have developed a tang to your voice that could be taken as the local brogue.' Annie noticed that he hadn't answered the question.

'What prompted you to move to these parts?' Kate stopped. 'Have I asked you that before?'

'Yes,' Adam nodded playfully. 'You have.' He topped up his glass. 'I came down here to live a different life. Where your survival depends on what you make of yourself. The locality was good and there was a cottage going very cheap with the land I wanted, so I took it.'

'And a damn fine job you have made of it,' remarked Annie, well in her cups.

'Thank you. We are much alike, you and I. Independent and self sufficient. You don't often find that in a young woman.' He paused. 'Not that I am saying that most women are less capable than a man. But most want to get married, have children, and then spend a great deal of the rest of their lives looking after others.'

'True enough. I never got the chance to get that far. My husband bugg … cleared off before then. Thank goodness.' Annie realised that she was burbling a little and looked at Kate for help.

'We both appear to be in the same position as far as marriage goes Adam.' Kate thought about expanding on her own life but didn't. Instead she casually asked Adam if he had ever been or contemplated marriage.

Adam was silent for what seemed an eternity. 'Marriage is not something that I have viewed as necessary. If two people are together and pledge that bond, then that is all that is required for a stable relationship. A piece of paper may say you are married, but your heart is the final witness to that.'

Both Annie and Kate thought long and hard about Adam's statement. It was right; they knew that, but both had been brought up to honour the sanctity of marriage through their respective childhood church teachings.

At the door both women shook hands with Adam. Neither contemplated that he would offer to touch their cheeks with his lips, but both yearned for a closer contact than his hand. Even so, the energy each felt as he squeezed their hands ricocheted through them like an electric current. It immobilised them as they watched the strong strides to the front gate.

'My goodness,' said Annie. 'My legs have gone all weak.'

'So have mine. Not felt like this since our schooldays.' Kate laughed to break the spell. 'And that was only over some pimply little fifth former with an overactive libido.'

Adam listened to the sound of helpless laughter as he turned toward his house. He also was inclined to laugh out loud and couldn't quite understand this new feeling he had.

Chapter Thirty Three

Detective Inspector Clare Baddeley weighed up the new evidence given to her by Kate MacManus over the telephone. 'Good work Kate. That's more than our lot have established. Now we know that there was a van in the vicinity, it could lead to a trail. I suspected that Angus might head north after trying to throw us on the wrong track. Now it looks a possibility. Mind you, it doesn't prove that the girl was snatched by the van owner, or that the van is in fact, Angus's. We have to work to eliminate the negatives and follow up the sighting. The local police are being very co-operative now that the two girls have disappeared on their patch.'

The inspector tried to follow the course of Angus's escape from the moment he fled the church, leaving the dead body of his Father Confessor meeting his lord long before he planned. She traced the route of the stolen car to the garage, leaving a false trail, to Lymm where another vehicle had been purchased. After that this had obviously been swapped for a camper van. The ideal transport for someone who did not want to book accommodation or be seen. Has he still got it? Was the van seen by the child, the one that Angus had purchased?

If it was another false trail, then we are running out of options, reflected Inspector Baddeley.

She had already authorised Kate to carry on with her investigations. Firstly to find the second girl who had most likely passed the van on her way home. Secondly to put out an all vehicle alert to find the camper van. Difficult in those surroundings where most of the mountainous countryside could hide an army.

Have we missed anything? She concentrated on putting herself in Angus's shoes. What did he need to survive? Money. Transport. Clothes. Change of appearance. Where would he get them?

Answer – another lock up.

Inspector Baddeley called her assistant, Detective Sergeant Jean Cropper. 'Have we raised any clues as to where MacManus might have had another stowaway place or like?'

Short and chunky, but with a puckish face, Detective Sergeant Cropper was efficient and quick witted. 'We are searching all the known rental properties of that kind within a perimeter of five miles. We are hoping that whatever storage he had, he would have wanted to be able to reach it fairly quickly for a situation like this. It is almost as if he was anticipated being caught out one day and had prepared for it.' She shook her head. 'Crafty blighter.'

'Yes. It would appear so. From his experience in the force he realised that he couldn't get away with it forever. Not with something like this. Too many of so-called "friends" might one day rat on him. Have a word with all known associates of MacManus and see if they know anything. He might have mentioned if he had a stash and the likely place.'

'Will do. By the way,' Cropper stopped at the door. 'That gun. The one that went missing on that raid. It has never been traced.' Her look reflected a grim reminder that MacManus might be armed.

'I am aware of that. Let's hope that we can catch him before he resorts to using it.'

After her sergeant had left, Clare jotted down a few ideas. Angus would definitely change his appearance. How? He had that distinctive sandy/ginger hair that would stand out in any crowd. Point one. Change hair colour. What to? Obviously darker. What else hid a face from view? Spectacles. He would choose heavy dark ones, they were the best distracter of the face behind them. So now we had a same size, can't do much about that, dark haired – spectacle wearer.

Photographs of him would not in themselves be much help to the local police. She noted to send a photofit of his new appearance to the search teams, together with a description of his van, if it was his. One important point also to warn them of. He most likely had a gun. And that he would be prepared to use it. Before his escape, his murders had been restricted to children. Now his priest had suffered the same fate as his other victims.

Let us pray that we get to him before he entices any more young girls into his wicked web. Inspector Baddeley crossed herself, a habit she had carried from her Catholic childhood, even though she had discarded the faith.

Chapter Thirty Four

So far, so good. As he expected it to be. Angus MacManus recognised that his planning had been good up to a point. He fully appreciated that the traces would be out and that he would, in time, be associated with the two girls in Scotland. They would automatically think it was him. Why can't any other girl snatcher be operating in other parts of the country he grinned? That would really throw them. But he couldn't risk being caught anywhere near where the two girls had vanished.

A change of plan. Kate could wait. He had to establish a safe area far away from Scotland. While the police were busy searching high and low, he could be sat comfortably watching the useless pursuit from a distance. When the activity died down, as it inevitably did, he could return and find Kate at his leisure. He already had a fair idea where she was located. Annie wouldn't have moved far from her previous home. Before he left Scotland he would have a word with the McBrides, especially that husband of Annie's. He wouldn't take much breaking when he got his hands on him.

Firstly he had to change his transport. The van was too much of a giveaway. He had learned that from his years in the force. Change frequently. Keep the police guessing just what vehicle they were looking for. That was the only lead they had. Someone, somewhere, would most likely have mentioned that a van had been seen in the vicinity of a school. The hunt would be on. Where to get rid of this van? The obvious answer was in one of the lochs. He would study the maps and find the deepest. The one with a sheer drop quite near the shore.

He consulted his road atlas and chose one closest to a ridge of mountains. They would undoubtedly continue down into the depths. If he could find a road or a track on a steep incline, then a push would see the van disappear forever.

Got it! Loch Monar to the west of Cromarty. A height of over 2000 feet with an escarpment plunging to 400 feet almost at the loch edge. All he had to do was find a suitable path to a high point.

The A831 would take him as far as Erchless Castle where a minor road followed the river Beauly all the way to Monar Lodge. From there it appeared that no road circumvented the eight mile S shaped loch. But there would be one. There always was.

The journey of just under forty miles took him two hours. He did not want to attract attention on the main road so kept to a respectable "tourist" speed.

Monar Lodge was a small community of about a hundred souls. It was a passing point for other tourists anxious to see the loch, one of the deepest in that part of the highlands.

He followed two other cars and a larger motorised caravan along what could only be called a dirt track. Eventually each one stopped along the side of the loch for one reason or another and Angus looked for any sort of trail up and away from the edge of the loch.

On the north side between Loch Mhuilich and Loch Monar, Angus found a side track up to what was probably some observation point. Exactly what he was after.

With difficulty and a few wheel slips he made it as far as some fifty feet or so above the water. Taking everything that could identify him, wiping the door and controls, he slammed the door and estimated the drop. He tied the steering wheel with rope into a central position and put the gear into neutral. It was now or never. He released the handbrake and jumped from the van, slamming the door as he did so.

Angus held his breath. The van ran straight down the track, gathering speed as it broke scrub and scattered shale in its wake. With a final surge, the van tumbled over the final bank of about ten feet and crashed into the loch. Still at first, it took an age to fill with water and then it sank quite quickly beneath the dark waters, sliding down to its last resting place.

Angus followed it down the track and looked left and right. No one in sight.

Heaving his rucksack onto his back he started to walk back the way he had come. A heavy hat and turned up collar hid whatever features anyone could have hoped to see. Hikers were frequently along this road and he was just another one enjoying the splendours of the Scottish countryside.

Angus passed two of the cars and their passengers picnicking by the loch. He didn't look at them and they didn't look at him.

He didn't fancy the long walk back, so looked for an opportunity at the rest stops along the way.

A lone figure was perched on a slight mound with binoculars to his eyes. Must have a car somewhere, reasoned Angus. And not too far away. The spot was not a recognised stopping spot, so Angus continued around an outcrop of rock. There it was! A Nissan. Easy as pie to break in. And to start. Within twenty seconds Angus was in the car and reaching for the ignition wires. The engine burst into life and Angus quickly reversed onto the road and was away. The innocent birdwatcher was intensely engrossed on tracking the antics of the Great Crested Grebe serenely gliding among the reeds wafting against the gentle current of the calm water.

Now that Angus had transport he could return to his previous locality, ditch the Nissan and procure a legal car which could not be traced.

Right! Detective Inspector Baddeley, follow that if you can. Angus laughed all the way to the nearest town.

By the time the car was reported stolen, Angus would be far away on his way back to England. There he would plan his move against Kate, and the retribution he would take against the despicable woman who had betrayed him.

Chapter Thirty Five.

He has been operating in the nearby lochs to Loch Garve. Sightings of him have been seen and there are two children missing. They may be down to him or just co-incidence. Search for him so that we can prepare for the duty we have to fulfil.

I am aware of this. I follow the newspapers and the reports on the radio. I have visited the other two lochs near where the children were reported missing, but found no trace of him. Perhaps he is lying low somewhere else. I will continue the search.

Good. He is the last renegade from the course we have set for the future. His destruction will free us from the barbaric rituals of the past. We can all live in peace as intended. As you are now. The success of your mission will be the culmination of a great rebirth of our natural ethics so wilfully destroyed by the antecedents of the one you seek.

Chapter Thirty Six

'I thought you might like to come with me to choose the gun you requested.' Adam stood on the doorstep with an innocent look masking any emotion he might be feeling.

Kate had answered the door and jumped as she was confronted with the last person she was expecting to see at this hour.

'I .. I was just having my breakfast, won't you come in?'

'Thank you. The place I have in mind is not too far from here. A gun dealer I have dealt with before. In Dingwall.' He stepped over the threshold. 'I have a small pickup now and can drive you there if you are free.'

Kate felt the tingling again. A sort of clutching at her chest and a quickening of her pulse. She hoped that it didn't show. Why do I always feel this way in his company? she asked herself.

She tried to hide the slight tremble in her hands as she ushered him through to the living room.

'Is Annie not here?' Adam said.

'No. She's out on her rounds.' Surely he noticed that the van was missing? Is that why he called out of the blue?

Adam sat on the sofa and crossed those beautifully honed legs. Kate had admired them every time he went running along the loch. Which was often.

'Tea?' she enquired.

'A glass of water if you have it please.'

Kate duly obliged and excused herself with a shrug of her shoulders indicating that she was going upstairs to dress. Until now she hadn't realised that she was in her dressing gown. Perfectly modest but not the sort she would have wanted him to see her in.

A quick change into some calf length trousers and a cashmere sweater made her presentable. Her hair was brushed back in a sweep behind her ears and fastened with a clip at the back. Perfect, she murmured. Then cursed when the lipstick broke. She removed the little she had put on.

'All present and correct sir,' she said as she bounced down the stairs.

Kate thought she saw a flash of appreciation cross Adam's face and then it was gone. Imagination, she murmured. I'm getting ahead of myself.

The journey to Dingwall was uneventful. Kate chatted about the countryside and was amazed with the store of knowledge that Adam had in the flora and fauna in abundance all around them. Like an encyclopaedia, she thought.

'You seem to know your way around these parts Adam. Do you come here often?' As soon as she said it she collapsed into uncontrollable laughter. 'I'm sorry,' she said. 'But that's about the crassiest chat up line that ever existed. It wasn't meant that way.'

Adam laughed with her but she wasn't sure if he understood the implication of the phrase. Highly intelligent in all manner of practical aspects of life, but unworldly in the nature of relationships with people. As if he had never had the benefit of the schooltime chatter that taught children so much about growing up. That was another question she would like to ask him. Which school did he go to? But that could wait. He was pointing out the beautiful waters of Loch Achonachie and the types of trees and shrubs which now forced their golden images onto the shimmering surface of the idealistic beauty spot.

'When were you here last?' asked Kate. She was aware that she was almost putting Adam under an interrogation with her usual approach to questioning. Must be a bit more subtle she promised herself. To compensate she added, 'I mean Annie and I were here not long ago, I think we told you.'

'Yes. I was here a little before that. At the beginning of the month I think. Then a week later I visited the other loch – Loch Bruicheach.'

Something rang a bell in Kate's head. "The beginning of the month?" That was about the time that the two girls had gone missing! Why am I thinking like this? I know it's all nonsense about the water horses but still something persists at the back of my mind. Too many tiny instances of where the image immediately jumps into the mind.

'Terrible wasn't it about the two girls. I can't imagine the anguish their parents must be going through.' She decided to confide in Adam of her "literary" enquiries of the first mother and how she had questioned Lesley's school chum. 'It was a camper van. Colour not really known, but it is a lead for the police. Might not be anything to do with it, but until it is proved otherwise, it remains the top of the list.'

'You sound as if you have a very investigative mind Kate. That is good. Knowledge is all powerful. If you get to write of your conclusions, then I shall look forward to reading the piece.' Adam turned his perfectly honed features to Kate and that weak feeling took over her knees and stomach once again.

What is it with me? I can't even sit here calmly and carry on a conversation with this man without feeling as if I want to grab him and hold him to me. Kate's thoughts chased around in her head without finding any logical explanation except that it was the sort of experience that young girls get as they reach puberty and go dotty over some heartbreaker.

She shook herself and blew her nose to hide her frustration.

'Got a cold coming on? I can turn up the heater if you wish.'

'No. I'm very warm thank you.' Kate couldn't tell Adam just how warm she really was and it wasn't in order for her to tell him exactly where she was feeling the warmth.

'Here we are,' said Adam as he parked the truck in the market square. 'The shop is just over in the corner.'

Kate noticed the window sporting all types of rifles and guns. Never see that in England, she thought, but in Scotland shooting was a major sport and didn't spawn the explosion of illegal shootings that some cities in England did.

At the sound of the doorbell the rather thin, bespectacled man with kindly eyes appeared and lifted his brows as he recognised Adam. 'Ah, the gent with the Winchester rifle. Satisfactory is it?' His smile confirming that he had noticed no rifle case for any sort of complaint.

'Perfect thank you,' said Adam. He indicated Kate as he asked if the shop had a suitable shotgun, not too heavy, for ordinary shooting purposes.

Can't tell him it's to keep off an ex-husband can we, smiled Kate. She kept her face straight as the man reached into a cupboard behind him and selected a BSA twin barrel type with breech loading. 'This will be most suitable for the young lady sir. Not too heavy and easy to operate.'

Kate couldn't help hiding a smile as she was accustomed to firearms with her police training during her earlier years. She was thankful for the "young lady" though.

Adam took the gun and rested it in his shoulder, making false shots around him. 'Here,' he said. 'You take it, handle it for some time to get used to its size and weight.'

Kate tucked the stock into her shoulder as she remembered and hoped to god that she would never have to use it. 'Fine,' she said.

'Good; we'll take it,' offered Adam. 'Same as before? A complementary box of shells?'

'Of course. No good without them is it?' chuckled the shopkeeper.

Riding back in the truck, Kate once again dwelt on the co-incidence of Adam being around the two lochs at the time as the missing girls. Why had he gone there? Surely not to admire the views? Had he some other purpose?

'You said to the shopkeeper "same as before." And he recognised you. Have you purchased a gun there recently?'

Adam nodded. 'Yes.'

'Whatever do you want a gun for? Not protection like we do surely?' Silly question really she reflected. Adam was just as likely to have burglars or raiders as Annie and she were.

'I use it for target practice. Away from any danger of hitting people' he assured her.

'Oh. Didn't know you liked that hobby.' A follow up struck her. 'Did you belong to any rifle clubs where you lived before?'

'No.'

Kate's face dropped as she was not allowed once again to peek into his past.

They rode in silence for some minutes until Kate asked him if he would give her lessons in shooting. 'I need some practice obviously. No use pointing a gun unless you intend to use it is it?' She made a joke of it. 'At least that is what all the cowboys said in the old westerns.'

Adam showed no sign of recognising the phrase.

'If you like. I could collect you and take you to a spot where we won't be disturbed.'

That's the best chat up line I've heard in many a year, Kate almost blurted out, but knew it would be lost on Adam. 'OK,' she said. 'Make it the day after tomorrow. I'm helping Annie on the stall tomorrow.'

'Bring some warm clothes. Do you wear spectacles at all?'

'Spectacles? Why?' said Kate.

'It is always safer to protect your eyes. There can be a bit of a backdraught. I can bring some goggles if you like.' Adam went on to explain the full workings of the shotgun and its capability.

'You know an awful lot about guns Adam. You weren't in the forces were you?' Kate kept probing, hoping that Adam would divulge some particle of his previous life. He didn't.

'I studied them from books. It fascinated me how hu .. people,' he quickly interjected, 'would want to devise something whereby one man could kill another.'

Kate knew he was being serious. Why did he trip up over saying humans? That was what she presumed he was going to say. 'You don't believe in killing any life then?'

'No. That is in the hands of the almighty. It is his prerogative, and his alone, to make a judgement.'

'But surely there are times when it is right to act on his behalf to prevent others killing you?'

This argument was getting deeper than she intended, but it might encourage Adam to reveal something of his own upbringing.

'Perhaps. But who decides which side is in the right?' Adam pulled the truck over to a lay-by and stopped the engine. 'I think if we are to continue this philosophical conversation, we should do it more pleasantly in the surroundings of nature. Come. There's a place I want to show you.'

Chapter Thirty Seven

Annie was busy in the kitchen listening to the 5 pm news on her new radio when there was a sudden announcement. "The police team leading the search for the girls, reported missing two weeks ago has just reported that Jeanette Steadman aged 13 has been found, safe and well in Glasgow. Apparently she was living in a slum with other girls but this morning walked into the Central Police Station. She is being checked by a local doctor, but is said to be "not suffering any noticeable harm." Further reports will be given as soon as there are any further developments. The other girl, Lesley Green, is still missing."

Poor little mite muttered Annie as she sat down with her morning coffee. Hope they find the other one now.

Where can Kate have got to with Adam? The question had been haunting her ever since Kate had left a note that he was taking her to buy a gun. Didn't take all this time surely? She didn't want to admit it, but she felt a little jealous that Kate was monopolising Adam lately. Can't another girl get a look in then? She scolded herself for her selfish attitude. Kate needed male company after what she had gone through.

Soon after her arrival, Kate had sat one night and talked to Annie. "I need to get this off my chest Annie," she said. "The whole damn lot in every detail. It haunts me at night and I can't look at a picture of a young girl without it reminding me of just what a monster Angus was." Her expression had drawn tight lines around her eyes and mouth. "And still is as far as I am aware."

Kate had opened her heart to her friend and confessed that the first person she thought of when she heard that two young girls were missing, was Angus. That's how deep the injury goes, she had reflected. The trauma she had suffered after the arrest was almost too much to bear, but she had held up until the trial and then the pain had hit her.

The first thing I should have noticed was the sex, she had said in a stilted, almost comatose manner. It changed. It no longer gave her the thrill as it used to. But that's how it is after the first few years of marriage isn't it? She talked to herself mainly as Annie listened.

But then one morning after Angus had gone to work she thought long and hard about it. He no longer wanted her! She could tell by the way he finished quickly and rolled away without a word. She had even offered to spice it up as they used to at first, but had had no encouragement.

Going through the male menopause, she had assumed. But sometimes she would catch a glint in his eye when youngsters were around. He started talking more to the next door but one neighbour's girl, who was coming up to senior school.

Kate saw the lustful look as he stood in the front garden watching the young girl pedal off to the High School.

All the signs were there, but she just hadn't connected with Angus.

She started to look through his drawers and his desk while he was on duty. The most guilty feeling I've had, she had blurted out to Annie. I wouldn't have wanted him to do the same to me. But she found what she was looking for.

It didn't seem incriminating. Just a list of the schools in the Manchester area. Most of them girl's schools. Might have been in connection with a case he was on. But wouldn't he have kept that under wraps with his official papers?

Then when a girl went missing from Withington High School, he was called into the missing persons team. Usually, three or four days is allowed before the search really gets under way. No force could spare the manpower to follow every reported missing person.

But this case was different. Her bicycle had been found on the outskirts of Withington park with her school satchel tangled in the handlebars.

Kate sobbed silently as she admitted that she didn't share her suspicions with anyone at the station. Well would you have done? she had asked Annie.

Angus had been always one for volunteering for extra duty and would come home after a day shift and announce that he had to go out again. A surveillance job, he had said. And that was truer than Kate had ever imagined. Watching young girls at play wherever he could find them.

One time she followed him, Kate said. He drove to the other side of Manchester to Prestwich where the local senior school had a good reputation for turning out bright pupils. It advertised for evening classes for students who wanted to do extra-curriculum subjects in addition to GCSE subjects.

Why was he going there? Kate wondered. As far as she knew, there wasn't any case in progress at the moment with any connection to the school.

'I watched him,' Kate related with a dead pan expression as if seeing it on a cinema screen. 'He parked a little way from the gates to the school and waited. The finishing time for the sessions was billed as 8.30pm. Late enough for most youngsters but in time to catch buses or be picked up by parents. One particular girl wearing a short gingham dress exited the gate and strode purposefully along the avenue as if she hadn't far to go.

'Angus's car moved. It trailed her slowly as she approached a turn in the road and overtook her, stopping just around the corner.' Kate gaze fixed on Annie. 'He knew her route and had obviously watched previously so that he could be in a position to wait for her.'

Kate's mouth felt dry as she wrestled with emotions. 'He slid over to the passenger seat and watched through his rear view mirror. I was on the other side of the road with my head below the window. His attention was on the girl and not on me. As she drew near, he opened the door, stepped out, and grabbed her, pinning her with his arms, putting something on her mouth. It was all over in a few seconds and he bundled her into the car, slamming the door. No one had seen him but me.'

'Here Kate, drink this,' said Annie, handing her a whisky. 'Take your time. Let it all come out.'

'Thank you Annie.' Kate was grateful for the pick-me-up and composed herself.

'He drove off and I contacted the station relating what I had seen. I did not tell them it was Angus at first. Then they asked how I had been in that vicinity in the first place. I said that I was looking at the schedule for a friend of mine. I was too ashamed to admit it. I had snitched on my husband. What wife does that?' Kate sat back in horror at the thought.

'If you hadn't, then the poor girl would have been the next on his list,' Annie interjected.

'You're right of course. I tracked him all the way to the countryside near Holcombe. A lonely place at night, but more frightening because I knew what was about to happen. When he stopped I gave the station the location and they relayed it to the squad cars. What bothered me was would they be in time? I couldn't risk them arriving after whatever Angus was going to do, so I left my car and followed him with the girl slung over his shoulder into a small spinney not far from the road.'

At this point Kate broke down and sobbed. 'I'm sorry,' she said. 'I can still picture it now.'

Annie gave her a few minutes. 'Go on Kate. You're nearly there.'

Kate took a deep breath and continued. 'He laid the young girl down and started to remove her clothing. I couldn't stand it any more. I charged in and started to hit him with my fists. He was so startled he didn't resist at first and then he grabbed me and hit me about the head. I went down. He was screaming all the time. Swearing and telling me it was all my fault. Nothing I did could pacify him. "It's not what you think," he yelled. "I wasn't going to hurt her."

I just lay there, my mind unable to connect this with my husband. Then he took a piece of rope out of his pocket and came toward me. I screamed as loud as I could but he was too strong for me. He stuffed a handkerchief in my mouth and bound me to a tree. "Now you can watch, you useless bitch and see how it's really done." He thought it was a game as he taunted me about watching him. He removed the rest of her clothes. "She'll be coming round in a minute then we can have some fun." I prayed that the girl would stay still but she came to quite quickly and started yelling. Angus slapped her and said if she didn't stop he would kill her there and then. There was a sudden rush of dark uniforms and bedlam before they got him under control. The poor little girl was almost comatose.'

The sweat broke out on Kate's brow and slowly dribbled its way down to her chin. 'The police had arrived just in time and arrested Angus. Angus was babbling by now, making all sorts of excuses, defiling my name and saying that the girl had come willingly.

'When I was able I told them the whole story. The suspicions, the evidence I had found at home, the late nights. They soon connected the other missing girls to Angus's movements on those days they had disappeared. What they had to do now, was to get him to admit that it was he who abducted them. And also where they were now.

'He clamped up completely. They charged him with the girl's abduction and attempted rape, but weren't able to get the confession they needed for the other two.

'That's where he slipped up,' Kate said. 'In a search of the house, we found a secret space behind one of his drawers that contained school photographs. Photographs of the two girls he ….. ' Kate had laughed cynically at that. 'Would you believe it? A copper keeping items connecting him with the crime. That's how distorted his bestial craving had driven his mind. After that he pleaded insanity and revealed where the bodies were buried.'

Annie broke off her recollections of Kate's trauma as she heard the front door latch.

'Hi Annie, I'm home.'

'Bout time too,' Annie said under her breath.

'Did you miss me?' said Kate, all bouncy with her eyes sparkling like they'd had a polish.

'Not particularly,' answered Annie. 'Been busy all day.'

Kate understood at once that Annie was playing it cool. 'Adam apologised for not coming in, but he had a busy evening in front of him.'

Annie went into the kitchen. At least he didn't take her home, that's one consolation. Must warn Kate about him. There was something that didn't ring true but she couldn't put her finger on it.

The telephone rang. 'I'll get it,' said Kate.

'Yes?'

'That's not Annie. Who are you?' The voice sounded abrupt and had an unpleasant tone.

'Who's speaking please?' Kate decided to ignore the insult.

'What's it to you? Put Annie on the phone.'

'Not until you tell me who is calling,' persisted Kate.

Annie came in from the kitchen mouthing "who is it?"

'Sod off,' said the voice and disconnected.

Kate told Annie of the conversation and described the voice and at once Annie knew who it was.

'Andy!' she moaned.

Chapter Thirty Eight

Detective Inspector Baddeley gathered her team in the conference room. A motley collection of characters and sizes. Male and female conjugating together to bring criminals to their just desserts. Only this one was proving particularly abhorrent.

The subject was Angus MacManus. Known to most in the room but many would admit that they didn't really know the man behind the façade. Hidden depths that shocked them all. Now he was on the run, with a further murder to add to his tally, there was an urge to capture him quickly.

They all looked to DI Baddeley to supply the answer.

'Angus MacManus,' she announced loudly, and pointed to his picture on the board. 'That is how we know him. Forget it. He will have changed. How we don't know but if we imagine how he would alter himself, what features would he add?' She looked at each face focused on hers. 'Go through your moments of contact with him and see if he ever fancied any other look.'

There was silence. Then one young Detective constable put up his hand. 'Yes?' said DI Baddeley.

'Some time ago he mentioned that he was fed up with people calling him "ginger nut" and sometimes wished he was dark. "I stand out too much. Couldn't commit a crime with hair like mine," he used to say.'

'Thank you Mike. Good point. My feelings exactly. He would go dark to hide his locks. What else? Any ideas?'

Most shouted "spectacles," or "moustache," or "beard."

'So,' nodded the inspector. 'Shall we add some of those to this photofit picture?' She took a dark hairline from the pile on the desk and placed it over the picture of MacManus. Then she added dark spectacles. 'Not the MacManus we all know is it?' Further additions brought a completely different man to the fore. 'Copies of these altered pictures will be given out to each of you. This is the person you are now looking for.'

Next she turned her attention to clothes. 'What did he wear out of uniform?'

'Usually a smart suit or jeans with a blouson,' said one.

'Let's take it that he won't be travelling in a suit.' Again she threw out a question. 'Did he like hats?'

'Wouldn't be seen dead in one,' shouted an old copper who had known him the longest. 'Best thing that ever happened to him was when he could chuck his police hat for good. That's what he said when he transferred to the investigation side.'

'So we have a man, same height, dressed in probably jeans and a blouson. Dark haired with spectacles and possibly a moustache or beard. Any other features that might give his identity away? Like mannerisms, walk, itches, facial movements?' The inspector took down each and every one of the suggestions coming from the floor. In the end a picture they could all work on emerged from the session.

'Now the most important issue. Where is he?' Inspector Baddeley didn't expect an answer and related the known movements of MacManus to date. 'He left the church at Gorton and stole a white Ford Cortina car. He tried to put off the scent with a conversation with a petrol station. At that time he was still a "ginger nut".' This brought a chuckle from the gathered throng. 'Although we haven't traced the car, a reliable source indicated that he purchased a further car, make unknown. From our further enquiries - good work Tom,' she nodded to a detective at the rear, 'we traced his lock up and there was enough stuff in there to set him up for a scenario like this. Money. So we know he had funds. Clothing, tools, a box of tints and dyes, but most importantly, no gun. We have reason to believe that he secreted a Walther PPK from a certain raid in which he was concerned.'

The room remained silent as the Inspector placed another photograph on the board. It was of a twelve year old girl. In school uniform. The second of the two missing girls from just over a week ago. 'We had presumed that MacManus was up to his tricks on the way north when reports of two missing girls were filed. Fortunately one has been found. The other is still missing. Maybe MacManus is not concerned with this one. We don't know. But it is in the bounds of possibility that he wouldn't wait long before his mania surfaced. Follow the trail, even if it leads nowhere. There are no other clues as to where he is. The Scottish police will all be issued with the descriptions you have before you.' She saw a few query the word "Scottish." 'The reason why we are concentrating on Scotland is that his ex wife Kate has taken a break from duties there. I can't tell you exactly because it is more than likely that MacManus will be going after her. We have already had a leak from this office as to Kate's absence of leave. It won't take long before MacManus puts two and two together and finds out that she is in Scotland.' Her eyes took on a steely glint. 'We have to get to MacManus before he gets to Kate or another child.' She slammed her fist on the table. 'Find him!'

Chapter Thirty Nine

Andy McBride came out of the newspaper shop lighting a cigarette. With the Scottish Herald tucked under his arm he made for the clapped out banger that he called his car.

A man on the opposite corner watched carefully as the car drove off. Just around the other corner, a Ford van was parked and the man jumped in, fired the engine and took off after the Nissan. It wasn't difficult to follow. Angus MacManus had had plenty of practice over the years.

Eventually the Nissan pulled into the front drive of a fairly large detached house just off the main road. The hedge hid a pleasant garden, with a double fronted post war building, shuttered against the stiff gales from the loch.

'Gotcha!' shouted Angus as he cruised by the property and sat about setting up a surveillance. "Never move on a suspect's house until you are sure of who, how many, and the sort of persons inside." Taught to him by an old timer, he had proved the point many times.

Over the next two hours, Angus saw a man and a woman, obviously husband and wife and a younger woman leave the premises. The bakers! he guessed.

Off to work at the old mill in Strathpeffer that had been converted into a bakehouse. Were there any others beside Andy McBride at home? Angus wondered. He gave it another hour and then walked slowly up the diagonally bricked pathway. The loud knocker reverberated throughout the house as Angus looked for signs of movement in the curtains.

'Who is it?' yelled a voice from behind the door.

'Police,' answered Angus. He had his warrant card ready.

The door opened slowly and as Angus showed his card, he walked into the hall saying, 'can I have a word sir?'

'Here, what's all this about? You can't just walk in here.'

'But I'm in sir,' said Angus.

Andy blustered and tried to prevent Angus from continuing into the house. Angus pushed by him and opened the first door on the right and said. 'Yes, this'll do fine.'

'I haven't done anything. What are you after?' Andy McBride was getting more and more agitated.

'If you haven't done anything, then you've nothing to hide have you,' stated Angus. 'Sit down.'

Andy sat, his knees quivering slightly. He had had a few brushes with the law, but nothing serious. A little cannabis, drunk a few times, disorderly behaviour, but that was par for the course around these parts.

'Now sir. I am going to ask you a few questions. Questions I know you have the answers to.' Angus paused to make sure that Andy was fully concentrated. 'You have a wife called Annie I believe.'

'Had. We divorced some time ago.' Andy looked sullen and bit his lip.

'Did she live with you here?'

'Yes. With my dad and mum and my sister.'

'I take it she doesn't live here now then?' Angus pretended to record the conversation in his notebook.

'No. She left. Went to live somewhere else. Never seen her since.'

'Are you sure you have had no contact since she left?' Angus's piercing eyes held Andy's in a grip that made him wilt under the gaze.

'Yes. Course I'm sure. Just left and never told anyone where she was going.' Andy almost spat. 'Bloody whore.'

'Why do you say that? Is that why she left? Was she playing around?'

Andy was confused. He didn't want to admit that it was he who had been playing around. Not to this copper. 'I don't know. She just left that's all.'

'And you have no idea of where she lives now?' Angus saw Andy hesitate. 'I'll ask you again. Have you had any contact with your former wife?'

'Well. I tried to ring her once but some strange bird answered the telephone. Probably got the wrong number. Can't remember how I got the number or who gave it to me.'

'Have you got the number now?'

'Somewhere. I noted it down on a fag packet. Might have thrown it away. I don't know do I?' He frantically searched his pockets then gave up as his hands came up empty. Perhaps I put the packet on a shelf somewhere in my room. I'll have a look.' He rose and Angus rose with him.

'I'll accompany you sir, if I may.'

Andy had no option and clumped up the stairs to a back bedroom. Untidy and a bit grubby with clothes strewn everywhere, Andy searched his bookshelf for the vital packet. 'Sorry. Can't find it.' He yelled in agony as Angus clamped his arms up his back into his shoulder blades.

'Sorry chum. You've got to do better than that. Where is it?'

Andy struggled but could not break the grip. 'All right, all right. I'll get it.' He nodded to the chest of drawers by his bed. 'It's in the top. Under my pants,' he gasped.

Frogmarching him over to the chest of drawers Angus pulled open the drawer. He rifled under the not too clean underwear and came up with a cigarette packet. 'Not too hard was it?' he grinned.

'What do you want her number for anyway?' squealed Andy.

'That's my business sonny. You are not to contact her or mention any of this to anyone, understand?' said Angus giving his arm one sharp jerk to emphasise his words.

'No. No, course I won't.'

Angus let him go.

'If you do see her, tell her I am willing to take her back. She's still mine you know. And I'll find her don't you fret.'

'Not before I do you miserable scrounger,' Angus muttered on his way back to his car.

Chapter Forty

How is the search going?

I'm narrowing it down. I know that he is not in Loch Garve. The other two lochs show signs of him but he does not stay long. There are many lochs in the vicinity and it is possible that he is moving from one to another. No more incidents have arisen, except the disappearance of two young girls. One has been found, but the other is still missing. I am keeping in touch with the situation with one of the women I told you about. She appears to be more than the writer she professes to be. She has an instinctive way of extracting information, which indicates specialist training.

Has she questioned you?

To some extent, but she has not shown any signs of awareness of our differences.

There are practically none.

Only in the fact that I appear to be lacking in the niceties of relations between people. This only comes with years of association and that is something that I cannot assimilate from books.

You are a quick learner and will soon adapt.

I think I am beginning to already. Strange feelings that I have not encountered before. And a contentment different to any I have experienced.

You are developing well. Keep in mind the first of your projects. Ensure you have the necessary equipment and the special chemical.

It is in hand.

Chapter Forty One

'So, what did you do all day then?'

Kate jumped at Annie's sharp question. 'We went for the gun as I told you, then he told me he had something to show me.'

'That's the most unlikely come on I've ever heard. Or the most direct,' giggled Annie as she relaxed from her previously haughty manner.

'You're only jealous,' said Kate teasing her friend. 'And I would be too. You needn't worry – nothing happened.'

'I should hope not! You hardly know him.' Annie made a grimace. 'At least you don't know him that well.'

'No. But at the same time I feel that he has been around far longer than he has. As if he has lived here all his life. Funny thing though.' Kate stared at Annie. 'He has never yet told of his parents; where he was brought up; his schooling; his youth. Anything.' She shook her head. 'Funny.'

'It's not funny. It's strange. No one cannot have a past. Or at least not talk about it. We've known him long enough to share at least some of his previous life.'

'That's the problem,' said Kate. 'He won't relax. Everything about him that is in the past is shuttered behind a steel wall. He'll talk for hours about nature and the wonders of the earth, the flora and fauna, as if he were a college professor. But I'll bottom him yet.' She paused. 'Sorry, that was an expression of my grannie. Used to describe a good clean of anything.'

'What did he show you then,' said Annie with a smile.

'He took me down to the loch and we walked until we came to a secluded spot …'

'Oh yes?'

'Not like that, you tease. No this was a small clearing that was not on view to any walker or any other vantage point. It was as if it didn't exist. Anyway he showed me some targets made out of sticks and brushwood. We walked away about thirty yards and he showed me how to hold the gun.' Kate laughed out loud. 'I didn't tell him that I had my shooting qualification from the force. I quite enjoyed his arms surrounding me and positioning the gun in my shoulder.'

'You're not fit to be let loose on any man Kate. Next you'll tell me that he taught you the prone position.'

'There you go again! But I must admit it was thrilling just to be held by him. He is so strong.'

'You are getting away from the point again. I take it you had target practice with your gun?'

Kate nodded. 'Not only that but he also showed me his rifle. A special one, he said. Then he demonstrated how he could knock off a single straw with one shot. He's even expert in that.'

'Nothing surprises me about Adam,' agreed Annie. 'The more I learn about him, the more I am convinced that he is not from around here. I would have heard of him years ago.'

'So that's all there is to tell.' Kate finished her cup of tea. 'Oh, one other thing. He invited us round for tea next Sunday.'

Annie exploded. 'You've kept the most important bit of news until now? I ought to belt you one. You're incorrigible.'

'At least he didn't invite me alone.' Kate laughed as she bounded upstairs. 'More's the pity!'

The telephone shrilled its annoying note.

'Yes?'

'Annie? No .. no. Don't switch off. I have something important to tell you.' Andy's voice sounded urgent.

'If this is another of your tricks, I don't want to know.' Annie's tone implied that she would cut him dead if what he stated wasn't genuine.

'I know you don't trust me but you must believe this.' There was a long pause then it all came out in a rush. 'I've been visited by the police. A detective I think. He wanted to know where you were living. As I didn't know I couldn't tell him. I wouldn't have anyway. But he come on to me like a bully and roughed me up a bit. He made me give him your telephone number. I couldn't help it Annie, I swear.'

'What force did he say he was from?'

'He didn't. Just flashed his warrant card at me and started asking questions. Why would the police be after you Annie?'

That's just what I'm wondering Annie thought. 'When was this and what did he look like?'

'Yesterday. About eleven in the morning. He was fairly tall, about five eleven I would think. Stocky build, dark haired with spectacles. His eyes were nearly black.' Andy listened to Annie breathing on the other end. 'He frightened me Annie.'

Annie was surprised at that. Andy didn't frighten easily. He was renowned for his aggressive attitude, but this man had scared him. What did the police want with her? And why approach Andy? Something didn't smell right.

'What else did he say?' Annie noticed Kate was standing beside her.

'Not much. Only that I was to keep this to myself and tell no one. But I had to warn you Annie. He seemed dangerous. A sort of wild look in his eyes.' Kate was listening in to the conversation.

Kate mouthed to Annie. 'Ask him what his voice was like.'

'Can you describe how he spoke Andy? His voice, do you remember that?'

Andy thought a moment. 'He spoke slightly northern, but not Scottish. It was kind of harsh and then soft all of a sudden. A bit like … like …' Andy searched for a comparison. 'Like that bloke who married Liz Taylor. Richard Burton – that's it.'

'Thank you Andy. I appreciate you telling me. But that doesn't give you a licence to ring me whenever you like. Only if he contacts you again are you to contact me.' Annie rang off.

'What do you make of that Kate? Did you hear it all?'

Kate shook her head. 'Not all of it, but enough to know that the man was no copper. Andy didn't get a good look at his warrant card. He didn't give a name, or why he was there. No. That man was no copper. At least not a present one.' She collapsed onto the settee. 'That was Angus MacManus. I'd know that description anywhere.'

Chapter Forty Two

Adam led his two black ponies along the path of Loch Garve. His muscular frame outlined against the dark of the stately pine trees whose thrusting branches threatened to behead all who walked beneath.

Kate watched from her vantage point on the high bank further south. Adam broke into a trot imitated by the ponies. He easily kept up with them and his pounding thighs lifted high, simulating those behind. What is it that attracts me to him? mused Kate. Certainly he is handsome in the most rugged way imaginable. His physique was honed to perfection. He had told her that he worked out every day on a beam in the stables and his care of his smallholding added to the more than ample work out. A man in every sense of the word. And yet. He was not worldly wise. He knew everything, but nothing of people and their vagaries, suspicions, jealousies, or any of the attributes learnt over the years of growing up.

It was as if he had been sheltered from the formative years of life.

He never talked of friends, relatives, other neighbours, or discussed the news of the day unless prompted.

During her visit, Kate had chatted on about everything under the sun to get a response. When she referred to the missing girls, Adam had lifted his head slightly and his eyes bored into hers. She decided then to tell him that she was investigating their disappearance and had been to see parents and school friends in an effort to find a clue as to their whereabouts.

Adam seemed concerned that they were missing. He said he had read about it in the newspapers, but couldn't add to anything that Kate had discovered.

But when Kate told him that a recently escaped paedophile was suspected, he nodded and his manner relaxed a little. He said that he hoped the authorities would catch him before any others suffered.

The drizzle obscured Kate's view slightly and she peered at the three forms, now galloping along the edge of the water. Then it happened. Adam turned abruptly and threw himself into the dark foreboding water and swam out almost to the centre. The ponies followed, splashing and thrashing their tails, their heads creating V shapes like the pleasure boats crossing the Moray Firth. Then as if a signal had been given, they all disappeared beneath the ripples.

Kate was astonished. Where had they gone? She waited for what seemed an age until at last, a head broke the surface. With vigorous overarm strokes the man swam strongly back to the shore. Adam stood, the rivulets from his body sprinkling the pathway. Then he turned and sprinted back they way they had come, shedding the last drops of the loch and drying in the morning air as the rain stopped.

Kate stood still as a statue so that no observer could see her against the lightening sky. Adam disappeared around the north end of the lock and was lost to view. Kate shook her head. What will Annie make of that? she reflected.

Or more importantly, what do I make of that?

And where were Adam's ponies?

Chapter Forty Three

What a pillock Annie married, laughed Angus. Couldn't keep it in his trousers, so she ditched him. Serve him right. He wasn't the sort who could fool anyone. Had practically offered no resistance when I cornered him. So much for his devotion to Annie. He had spilled her telephone number like water out of a tap.

Now that Angus had the number, he had to find the address. He believed Andy when he said that he didn't know where Annie lived. He also didn't appear to know if anyone else was living with her.

Angus went to the local council offices in Inverness. The largest city outside of Edinburgh and Glasgow. There he asked to see the electoral role. 'When was this last compiled?' he asked.

'Three years ago before the elections for the County Council,' was the answer.

'And this covers the area north of here does it?'

The clerk looked at him with a bored expression. 'Aye. As far north as anyone would want to go. Mind you,' he frowned. 'That does'ne include the islands. They're under a separate authority.'

I'm not interested in the islands you stupid berk, thought Angus. 'Could I see them please?'

'Follow me. They're all on micro fiche if you know what that is,' the clerk said importantly.

I think we invented those in England, Angus was tempted to say but trailed along dutifully.

'Here's the machine. Just use the side controls to whistle through the pages as you wish.'

'Thank you,' said Angus and set to work to find Annie's name.

It took him about fifteen minutes to locate the name Annie McBride. The address given was the house where he had accosted her useless ex-husband.

'Damn,' he swore and slammed the machine with his fist. The look from the clerk was returned with a ferocious glare that stopped the words in the clerk's mouth.

Next the library. A search of their records was as useless as the first search. He left the startled librarian in a state of tremors as he demanded to see the membership list, thrusting his warrant card under her nose.

Where to next? What did Annie do? What was she interested in? He thought hard and long over a whisky in the Boar's Head. Nothing came to mind. He regretted that he hadn't paid more attention to Kate whenever she talked of her old friend. Or listened to the content of Annie's letters which arrived from time to time.

Perhaps he could ask around in the locations nearest to the Bakery house. That might be risky, but it was worth a try. Another dead end. No one admitted knowing where Annie had gone. She was there one day, the next she was gone, was the trotted out reply.

Estate agents. That was the answer! She must be living somewhere and where else would she get a house, to buy, or more likely to rent. She wouldn't have much money of her own so rental it was. Where to start first?

The largest town around and within striking distance of the Bakery house. Strathpeffer was the likely town. South on the A835 then onto the A834. Not very far and ideal for anyone wanting to rent within a reasonable distance.

The local Yellow Pages revealed that there were only two estate agents in Strathpeffer. One in a chain prominent throughout the Easter Ross and Cromarty region. If they were as efficient as they professed to be, then they would have records of property that they no doubt handled for their landlord clients.

'Yes sir, what can I do for you?' The small, bespectacled man looked up from his cluttered desk as Angus walked in.

'I am trying to trace a friend of mine.' Angus decided not to use the police approach as this man was not as gullible as the others he'd used it on. 'She was living just north of here at Heights of Brae. At the house owned by the McBride Bakery company. You no doubt know them.'

'Ach. Very well. Everyone around here knows the family. Well respected in the area and a good friend of the community.' The agent preened himself as if knowing the family attached some importance to himself.

'Yes, so I understand,' said Angus. But not the son that has turned out to be a right useless piece of garbage, he thought. 'One of the sons, Andy I believe his name is, is married isn't he? A girl from England I heard. Her name would be Annie McBride, but I know her as Annie Chambers. That's the girl I'm looking for. Known her for years but lost touch with her some time ago.'

'Aye. She ran away I am told. Terrible loss to the family. That poor wee laddie. Not married but for the wink of an eye and she ups and leaves him.' He shook his head and his wispy hair waved about his balding pate. 'Not enough discipline if you ask me. Too soft with them at the beginning. Now if it were ....'

'Yes I'm sure. I totally agree with you,' Angus butted in, not wanting to go into the rights and wrongs of marital bliss. 'But I need to see Annie because her mother back in England is very ill and Annie hasn't contacted her in almost twelve months. It'd be tragic if she were to die without saying goodbye to her only daughter.'

'Oh the poor wee lassie,' the agent again commiserated with Angus. 'Sure I'd tell you where she was living if I knew. Like I said. All I know is she ran off and that was the last anyone heard of her. Perhaps she went back to England. Most of them do you know.'

'So you didn't rent any property to her then?' Angus came straight to the point.

'I did not,' said the agent emphatically. 'And if she'd asked me, I would'ne have rented her one either!'

Angus left the shop and walked to the other estate agent on the opposite side of the town square.

A wholly owned private business, the agents had been a feature of the town for over fifty years. The proprietor who started it was still in charge.

Angus anticipated that this was where Annie would have gone. He was not wrong.

'Annie McBride you say.' The elderly agent pondered. 'A very well known name in these parts. Would she be part of the bakery family?'

'Yes. She married the son Andy.'

'Aye I remember it well. The young do all sorts of foolish things don't they? Then live to regret it. Nice girl. Far too innocent for the life up here.' He brushed his thinning hair away from his heavily lined forehead. 'Pity. Great pity.'

'Did you rent a place for her?' Angus was anxious to be gone. He had spent too long in the man's company. He would remember him if questioned.

'Aye. We did. A lovely little cottage way down by the loch. Good rent too. The owner is a little old lady who just wants a small income for her needs.'

'Do you have the address?' asked Angus.

'Aye of course we do. Rent paid as regular as clockwork. As it should be,' he added knowingly.

'Could you give it to me please. I'm very anxious to find her. Her mother is very ill and is worried that she won't see her before .. well, you know.' Angus told the same story as it had impressed the first agent.

'Deary me. What a sad tale. I do hope that you're not too late. Let me see if I can find it for you.' He went to his storage unit where hundreds of cards in a rotary wheel type of system were kept. Spinning the wheel he came to the "Mc" titles. 'There are quite a few of these,' he joked.

Angus didn't laugh. He was near to finding the place where he knew his ex wife would be holed up. The final piece he needed to recompense her for her betrayal. It never occurred to him that he was the ultimate betrayer in that he had hidden his dreadful secret from Kate for years.

'Ah, here it is. The agent took the card from the run and set it down on the desk. 'Annie McBride. Spinster.' He looked up. Makes her sound old doesn't it? But as I remember, she was still a striking young woman. Should make a man a good wife some day.' He shrugged. 'That is if she ever marries again.'

Angus copied the address into his diary. 'By the loch did you say? Which loch would that be?'

'Loch Garve. Not the prettiest, but nevertheless a sight to behold on a cold winter morning.' He frowned. 'Take care if you venture near that loch. It has a strange reputation. And not without cause either. It is said that a kelpie resides there. So keep your distance.'

Angus ignored the old man's warning. He didn't know what he was talking about anyway. He had the address. That was the important point.

Chapter Forty Four

Kate was determined to get to the bottom of what she had witnessed. She had related the whole story to Annie, whose incredulous face had a touch of the non believers.

'It's true I tell you.' Kate insisted. 'Adam went into the water with his ponies, disappeared and then re-surfaced and ran back to his house alone.'

'So what happened to the ponies?' Annie's sceptical tone told Kate that she was not fully supportive of the tale.

'I don't know. They never surfaced as far as I could tell. Anyway, there aren't many horses that submerge as far as I know.' Kate sat back and crossed her arms.

'Not unless they drown. And Adam wouldn't let that happen.' Annie thought for a moment. 'What was he doing with them in the water anyway? A short walk along the shore – OK, but not a swim like it was a day out.'

'You're right. We must put it to him. In a round about way of course. Wouldn't want to think that we have been spying on him,' Kate cautioned.

'That you've been spying on him. You seem to spend half your life looking out of the window in the hope of catching sight of him.' Annie let out a loud guffaw. 'Not that I blame you. If I had the time I'd do the same thing.'

'When are we going for tea then?' Kate asked.

'Tomorrow. Sunday. He invited us to go at about three o'clock. That should give us plenty of opportunity to fathom out what he was doing. Also we can check to see if the ponies are there.'

Kate nodded. 'I feel it in my bones that he is trying to accustom himself to the ways of a community. He is a lot easier to talk to now, but he is still a fount of knowledge with no interaction with people. Like he's been away for years with no contact.' Kate punched the air. 'Perhaps that's it. In prison, or on a desert island, or a hermit somewhere!'

'You're getting too fanciful for words Kate. It's this pretending that you are a journalist that is rubbing off on you. You don't want the truth, you want a fairy story. One where you end up on a desert island with your lover, like Adam, and live happily ever after.'

The girls chuckled with delight at the picture they were painting. Annie said between giggles, 'I wouldn't mind being shacked up with Adam anywhere. Just give me the chance.'

When Kate had calmed down she queried the statement. 'Would you really go that far with Adam?'

Annie thought a moment, then solemnly said. 'Of course not – only if he asked me!'

The morning was spent on the household chores and tidying the garden.

Kate was on the front lawn when Ailsa Morrisey trudged past with her shopping trolley. Where she was going, Kate couldn't guess. 'Hi there! How are you?'

Ailsa looked up and stopped. 'I'm going down to the loch. I need some wood for my fire. Coal's too dear.'

'It's a long way down there. Do you want me to help you?'

Ailsa looked at Kate. 'I can manage quite well on my own, but thanks for the thought.'

'Any more news of Craggy?' Kate was aware that the search had been dropped as was the usual pattern with missing persons. The first week or so, it was all hustle and bustle, then the media didn't want to know, people put it to the back of their minds, and it was laid to rest.

'No. Poor sod. Gone and nobody cares any more.' She bit her tongue. 'I do. And I'll keep looking for as long as it takes.'

'What do you think happened to him Ailsa?'

She raised her dark sunken eyes to Kate. 'Do you really want to know?'

'Yes.'

'The kelpie. That's the one that's got him. I told him to be careful, but he wouldn't listen. "Won't touch me," he used to say. "I'm too long in the tooth. Besides, I've lived next to his place all these years and he's never so much as shown his face."'

Kate shook her head. 'Well you take care yourself. Don't want another missing person in the news.'

Kate was about to go back in the house when Ailsa said. 'Like the little girl you mean.'

'Well .. yes. But that was probably an abduction by a man. It had all the signs of a paedophile type of crime.'

'What do you know about crime? A girl goes missing and all the newspapers immediately assume that some man has been responsible. They need to open their eyes to the facts. People have gone missing for years around here, but it is always put down to some recognisable excuse or other. Mark my words young woman. It'll happen again. Then perhaps someone will take notice.'

Ailsa pushed off with her trolley, muttering to herself and shaking her shaggy grey hair drooping down in long tangles over her hunched shoulders.

Kate thought long and hard about what Ailsa had said. Could she be right? Why did I automatically think of Angus at the time? One girl had been found. What if Angus had nothing to do with the other girl?

Then she remembered the telephone call from Andy. Angus was in the area, she was convinced of that. But who or what had taken the girl, she didn't know.

Chapter Forty Five

The search for Angus MacManus was going nowhere. The media were all over the police in that it was perceived that nothing was being done. Detective Inspector Baddeley herself had actually been hauled over the coals by her superior, despite the common knowledge that it was not primarily a problem of her particular station. Only that he had been on the force there and had connections to the officers. The Chief had been informed that all available officers north of the border were on the lookout for MacManus. That was where he is, had insisted the Detective Inspector. He had already committed a further offence according to Kate MacManus. She was certain that the trade marks were those of her ex-husband.

'How can she be sure?' The question was almost brutal.

'Because she knows him. She lived with him and was the major factor in his arrest. She studied his methods during the trial and connected him with both murders. They were the same MO. I could quote that leopards never change their spots. In this case I believe that Detective Sergeant MacManus is right.' Baddeley crossed her fingers and prayed that her faith was justly placed.

'Have there been any sightings of his transport? A camper van you said.' The Chief was sceptical of Baddeley's avenue of enquiry.

'A van was seen at the scene of the second girl's abduction from outside her school.'

'But not since.' It was a statement not a question.

'No sir. The territory around that part of Scotland is wild. You could hide an army for months.' As soon as Baddeley said it, she regretted it.

'We are not looking for an army inspector. Just one man and his camper van.' His tone indicated that the interview was finished, but Baddeley had an ace up her sleeve.

'We believe that he has been seen around the upper Cromarty area. Mrs MacManus reported that a man, more than likely her ex-husband had approached the ex-husband of her friend demanding her address. That would seem to indicate that he is searching for his ex wife: a move we anticipated. He wants revenge and Kate MacManus is the bait that may draw him out. He will get the address, he's good. And when he does, he will pay her a visit.'

'Have we a description? You have issued a photokit picture to all the forces involved. How accurate is this?' He was still sceptical of Baddeley's line of investigation.

'From the description given by this man, Kate's friend's ex, it fits the profile that we guessed he would take.' By way of explanation Baddeley added. 'There wasn't much else he could do to hide that golden crown of his.'

The Chief looked at his notes. 'Do you think we ought to send someone up there?'

'We already have Kate sir. She is working unofficially, but her reports are invaluable to our search. She realises the danger she is in, but is capable and as they say, forewarned is forearmed.' She decided not to tell him that Kate had a firearm for protection. Or apprehension she thought to herself.

'Very well. But keep at it. The personnel at this station feel responsible and I don't want any more tragic incidents on our record.'

Tragic incidents. Not a phrase I would have used, thought Baddeley. Bloody heinous murders more like.

She returned to her office and picked up the telephone. She had a feeling in her bones that MacManus would not leave it too long before he dealt with Kate. Let us hope that she keeps alert to the danger.

Another thought struck her. Now he knew Kate's address, might he be tempted to indulge in his favourite sport before the ultimate revenge he sought?

Kate answered immediately the phone rang. 'Yes?' She was wary after Andy's warning. 'Who's speaking please?'

'It's me Kate. Detective Inspector Baddeley. I'm trying to bring my information up to date on Angus. I've just had a rollocking from the Chief and I need to show him that we have progressed since my last talk with you.'

'Good to talk to you Clare.' Kate was more at ease using first names. Inspector Baddeley didn't object. 'You know that I have purchased a shotgun. A friend nearby has taught me how to use it, although I thought I was pretty proficient already. Angus hasn't contacted me directly. Yet. But he will, I know it. If he has the telephone number then he will have the address by now. Annie, that's my friend, and I are prepared. One thing worries me. We assume that he has a camper van or similar. One was seen very near the school where the second girl was snatched. Could have been him. Could have been an innocent camper. We don't know. I am going to have a look at the spot where it was seen. Might show up something, you never know. The police up here have organised a search force, in plain clothes to tour the area looking for the van. Until we find that we are stumped. There's an awful lot of empty space in Scotland. He could be anywhere. I am trying desperately to think of where he might be seen. Newsagents, he would try and keep himself up to date with the news. Pubs. They have TVs and this again will attract him. Food shops. He has to eat.'

'That's good Kate. One thought has struck me. How would he go about learning your address?'

'His first approach would be the electoral role. Residents in the local council list. Rental agencies. Estate agents. These are the places I plan to visit over the next few days. That's the way I would go about it.' Kate thought to herself that she would ask Annie who dealt with her rent. That would be the place Angus would be seeking.

'This friend of yours. You say that he is a neighbour? Could he be of any assistance if Angus does put in an appearance. I don't fancy you tackling him on your own. He's more than a match for you. And for Annie I would say.'

'Good question. We are going to tea this Sunday and I will test the water to see if he has any ideas about an early warning system.' Kate had had in mind to approach Adam and confide in him as to their present danger. Both she and Annie would feel much more confident if they knew they could rely on Adam to help, should the need arise.

'Keep me up to date Kate. And I will do the same from this end. Another search of your house is to be mounted to see if we missed anything. Bye for now.' The inspector rang off and Kate was left feeling more vulnerable than ever.

What if Angus came to the house when I'm alone? thought Kate. She made a note to mention to Annie that from now on, they lived and worked together. Four eyes are better than two. Six if she counted Adam's.

Chapter Forty Six

The lone cyclist pedalled slowly along the loch road. Fully protected against the weather with an old army cape and a waterproof hat, he struggled to maintain momentum against the northerly gale force wind. Little could be seen of his face, protected from the biting wind by a muffler.

No one saw him and he saw no one. The old bicycle ground its way through the puddles, swishing all aside as it made its way past the few houses and cottages that fronted the loch.

Angus MacManus kept a keen eye open for the house he wanted. It shouldn't be difficult to find. Set in its own small plot sheltered from the west by the steep cliffs behind it.

Annie's house. That's where she'll be holed up, I'm sure of it, he smirked. Thinks she's safe in this remote place does she? No one's safe from me. His thoughts turned to how he was going to get Kate on her own. He would have to keep watch somehow and log her movements and Annie's so that he could have all the time he needed to teach her the lesson she deserved. He was good at that. None of the girls knew what hit them when he was ready to grab them. Good planning. That's what gets results.

Through the blinding rain he saw the house. Couldn't be any other. There wasn't another within two hundred yards. Easy, he thought. No particular security measures. An old easy to break in type of house that had never had to withstand burglars or any other intruder.

There was plenty of natural cover on the opposite side of the road. A man could lie all day in the heather and the scrub and no one would be any the wiser. Wait for the weather to improve, then I'll take up my position and plan my moves. The ideas came thick and fast in his head as he pictured the scenario. How many times had he done this before?

The last time was with the little girl from the school further south. Perfect snatch. Over in five seconds. The only risk was the camper van. Someone may have seen it parked. But who would know the owner? Angus asked himself all the questions and was satisfied with the answers. Nevertheless he had hidden his present van and taken a bike from the small town nearby. No one would miss it straight away. It was outside a temperance meeting and those could go on for ever. He could picture the scene when the owner reported it to the police. A bicycle not worth two pence let alone worth pinching. Who'd do a thing like that? A prank most likely, by the youngsters out and about on a Saturday. The police would dismiss it and tell him to wait until it turned up in a brook or in a side street when the youngster had had enough of it.

The house looked deserted. It was a Saturday. Probably at the market. Perhaps I'll see if I can spot Kate there.

Angus had learned that Annie ran a kind of market stall with all manner of bric-a-brac and useful items. Kate would be sure to be lending her a hand. He could observe her from a distance and wallow in the satisfaction of knowing that he could strike whenever he wanted.

He heaved on the pedals, cursing the owner for not oiling the damn thing more often. Further down the road he passed another cottage. Neat and set back with far more land than the cottage deserved. A smallholder no doubt. Again no sign of life was apparent. Stables at the back and cultivated acres of produce just finishing for the season.

Keeping his head down, he pushed hard and mounted the small incline that took him to the outskirts of the adjacent village.

From an upper window in the cottage a pair of very dark unblinking eyes watched his progress with more than curiosity. The man noted the behaviour of the cyclist. He was surveying the area, that was apparent.

He tripped lightly down the stairs and put on his sou'wester and hat. Then he strode out of the cottage and took a gentle jog with no effort against the darkening skies. It would not take long to catch the reluctant cyclist.

Chapter Forty Seven

'Hurry up Kate, we'll be late for our date.' Annie's urgent call from down below disturbed Kate's thoughts about the threatening circumstances that had arisen over the past few days. Angus on the loose, and in the vicinity. Adam's odd behaviour with his ponies and the doubt that still existed about his background. She was certain that he was true to his ethics and would do anything he could to help them. But. She demurred over his reticence to confide in her. This would be a good opportunity to get him to open up.

'Coming Annie. Just got to get my hair in a presentable state.' Since coming to Scotland, Kate had had difficulty in keeping it in trim. The wild air and constant storms played havoc with it. In the end she had surrendered to the climate and just let it fall naturally to her shoulders. Anyway who around here would take any notice? Kate shook her head. Adam of course. Or would he?

Kate skipped downstairs like a teenager. Adam had that effect on her. She would dearly like to see Adam on her own, but that wouldn't be fair on Annie. Although Annie had professed to being dotty about Adam, somehow it didn't ring true. Not her type. She was just putting on a swagger as they used to in the old days at school.

Perhaps the opportunity would come to invite Adam to take her out somewhere. He enthused in showing her "his domain" as she called it. He knew the territory better than she did and especially the nearby lochs.

Adam was the perfect host as they sat down to tea beside the small window overlooking the loch. All fresh cakes and exquisite sandwiches with a teapot full of refreshing tea.

'Where did you learn to cook like this Adam?' asked Annie.

'There are a lot of books in the library and hosts of recipes in the magazines. It is like most arts. Easily accomplished if you follow the instructions.' Adam brushed it aside as it were of no consequence.

'Most women would die for a chef like you,' teased Annie. Then daringly fluttered her eyelids at him. 'Has no one ever told you that?'

Adam ignored the barb. 'I would think that being able to cook would not be the prime factor in attracting a lady. That is usually their preserve isn't it?'

'It certainly isn't mine Adam,' said Kate. 'I can cook, but no one would call it exceptional.'

'But if you learn the basics then the flavours will come naturally.' Adam's gaze held Kate in a sort of mesmeric state as she suddenly became aware that she was staring into those liquid dark pools that so fascinated her.

'I do my best,' stuttered Kate. 'I don't have to worry too much now though. There's only Annie to complain when I cook dinner.' As soon as she had said it she realised that she had let slip that it was part of her previous life.

Adam eyes smiled beneath the brows knitted together in understanding. 'I'm sure you are a very good cook. Perhaps we can learn from each other.'

Kate's knees went wobbly under the table and Annie flashed her a look that said "you've cracked it girl!"

All Kate could do was answer that she'd be privileged to watch him prepare a meal.

'Tomorrow then?' Adam said. 'I have a morning free if you'd care to join me.'

Before Kate could answer, Annie asked him. 'What do you actually do Adam? You've never said.'

There was a pause. 'I am a conserver of nature I suppose. I look after the environment. Ecology is a favourite subject of mine. I study the effects to alien elements on the various habitats in the countryside.'

'Sounds very important. And vital too. Too much destruction of the flora and fauna are allowed to take place. The lakes and the forests are all suffering from human interference.' Kate surprised herself with her sudden thoughts. 'Do you know I've never voiced that opinion so strongly before. Perhaps that's the problem. No one actually does anything about what they really feel.'

'Exactly,' said Adam. Again that piercing look caught Kate unawares and she tried not to blush. But she did.

'Well that was a revelation wasn't it Kate? You really impressed him with all that ecology talk. Was that just a come on?'

'No! Course it wasn't. I really do feel that strongly about the countryside. It's just that Adam has that effect on me. I have to speak as I feel.'

'He has that effect on me too, but it is you he has invited to breakfast tomorrow,' Annie said ruefully.

'You can come if you want.'

'Not a dog's chance. You go and enjoy the experience. I've got enough on my plate.'

'But what about our plan to stay together at all times?' Annie's reminder jolted Kate into an apprehensive mood again.

'Where will you be while I'm at Adam's?'

'At the market. Among hundreds of people. Can't touch me there can he?' You're the one he's after so just you be wary and let Adam walk you home afterwards. I shall be back about one o'clock.'

Chapter Forty Eight

Kate put on a simple dress for her visit to Adam. Simple cotton pulled in at the waist – she congratulated herself that she still had one – with simple low heeled court shoes over her sheer nylon tights. Thank goodness the suspender age had all but gone. But they did add a little spice to proceedings, she smiled.

He greeted her at the door and offered her a coffee. Deliciously strong and flavoursome. As I'd expect it, she told him. He laughed. Something caught in her throat and flashed down her to her stomach as she watched his body relax onto the sofa.

'This morning I thought we'd have a look around the land at the back if you don't mind. I can show you where all the various herbs and spices I use are growing. If you want the best, you have to use the best. And the best blends will give you the best experience you have ever had.'

'Good idea. I don't know a lot about all the flavourings the professional chefs talk about. Or how to blend them to get the best taste.' Kate realised that Adam was not entirely talking about flavours when he talked of "best experience." It raised her pulse another notch.

Both felt the tension between them. It was as if an electrical current held them in thrall.

The land was exceptional. Bereft of the summer vegetables but ploughed and fresh and ready for the coming spring. To one side was the herb garden. Every conceivable seasoning was on view.

Kate said. 'However do you cope with all these Adam?'

'Easily. I label them and over time I have identified most of them. One sniff and you know the effect it will have on a meal.' He turned to her. 'Like a woman's perfume. It is meant to attract the male is it not?' He half smiled. 'Like many animals, it is infectious and is in the order of things. It has been employed since the beginning of time.'

Kate had sprayed a rather modest amount of Chanel Number 5 on before setting out. He had detected it immediately. Again a shy sort of blush crossed her face.

'Did you know that some animals blush? It is natural when you are feeling a little nervous.'

'I'm not really nervous. It's just that .... that .... I want so to communicate with you but there is a barrier.' Kate stopped. 'I'm sorry, I didn't mean that to come out the way it did.'

'Of course there is a barrier, because neither of us has been fully truthful with each other.'

Kate blanched. Had he spotted that she was not what she professed to be? 'Perhaps I should be honest with you. I myself, feel a bit of a sham for not telling the whole truth.'

'Let us go inside. We shall be able to feel much easier with each other.'

They walked slowly to the back door. 'How are the ponies?' Kate remarked as they passed the stables. She tried to distract her mind from the unnatural breathlessness that was gripping her.

'They are fine. In the best of health really. I took them for a swim the other day. They loved it.'

At least he didn't try to cover that up, thought Kate.

'First things first. I don't think you came here especially for the cooking lesson. Although that offer is still open if you wish.'

Kate remained silent.

'There has been a growing familiarity between us for some time. That is good and I have felt the need inside me too. We are attracted to each other. Why, is a conundrum that is never really explained. Outward appearances are very important so everyone tells us, but it is the inner personality that clinches why two people merge together.'

Kate sat fascinated by Adam's logic. What was he about to tell her?

'I cannot go into the detail of my background but it is one of being sheltered from the world as the media tries to paint it. I have had to learn how to assess people and judge them, not on what their appearance is, but on what I feel in my subconscious.'

Adam saw Kate trying to comprehend what he was explaining. 'A simple way to look at it is when two completely blind people meet and fall in love. How do they assess the other? By contacting the mind, the inner part of us that is really the entity behind the façade.'

Kate had never thought of it like that. All her life she had been manoeuvred into the outward attractiveness of men. Then had come the investigation into their character. Could the initial attraction overcome any faults subsequently found in the so called "perfect partner?" She nodded. 'In my case that is entirely true.'

'How do you mean?' Adam raised his head waiting for the answer.

Kate took a deep breath. 'I have been married.' She looked at Adam to judge his reaction. There was none. 'I was married to a man who I thought was right for me. Later on it turned out that he was not the man I thought he was.'

Adam said gently. 'Go on.'

'Well, the first few years of marriage were conventional enough. I thought that the life we lived was enough. Both busy and committed to a nice home in Manchester. But it wasn't enough.' Kate faltered and Adam took her hand. It felt good. She hadn't noticed that he had moved closer to her as she spoke. It gave her the courage she needed.

'Both of us were in the police. We were both detective sergeants. I was, in fact I still am, a detective. I have taken compassionate leave after the discovery that my husband was a child molester and killer.' There she'd said it and it was a relief she felt at being so at ease with Adam.

'That must have been very traumatic.' He held her hand more tightly. She felt on the verge of tears. 'Let it go if you wish. I've a very willing shoulder to cry on.'

Kate let all her angst out in one long sob and gratefully sought Adam's arms for comfort.

After a while, she looked up at him and through her tears she saw the look that she had wanted for so long. A look of caring. Of a love of one being to another. There was no mistaking it. She wanted him to kiss her but he tenderly brushed the tears away from under her eyes and held her close. 'Tell me all of it.'

Kate related everything from the moment she had trapped him to the moment he had been sentenced to life imprisonment. Adam saw there was more to come and pulled her closer.

'He escaped a few weeks ago and I believe that he is in the area. That is why I wanted the gun.' She curled herself into his protective arms and trembled at the thought of Angus roaming the district. 'He has killed again and I believe he is responsible for the missing girl.' Gradually the shaking subsided and she lay content against Adam's body.

'He will not harm you, I promise.' He pulled her up and raised her head. His lips sought hers and found a willing, soft mound of warmth that even Kate didn't know she possessed.

A flush of excitement replaced the tremors of before and her body began to respond to the urge that she had felt ever since the first time she had seen Adam.

His kisses became more urgent and Kate now felt that this man was at last giving in to his inner feelings. His strong arms encircled her and lifted her from the settee and still locked in that electrifying kiss, he carried her to the bedroom.

Kate went willingly. There was no turning back. Her needs wouldn't let her.

He gently undressed her, slipping the cotton dress down over her shoulders and removing the underwear as if tending to a helpless woman. His clothes were shed just as quickly until he stood before her and she before him.

There was no embarrassment. They came together naturally and he held her so closely that she became part of him. She felt him against her and pulled him down onto the large double bed.

He unhurriedly stroked her and kissed her body. First the now thrusting breasts then the heaving stomach, twitching beneath him. His first touch of her dark pubic hair jolted her into spasms that she fought to control. He relaxed her and lay beside her until she calmed. Then he reached for her and lifted her on top of him and gently lowered her on to his waiting passion.

They were complete. The movement was like a symphony, played out to the full mind-blowing crescendo of a concert orchestra. Every nerve and sinew of her body co-ordinated in the most beautiful culmination of all that she had ever yearned for.

Exhausted and gasping at the enormity of it all, Kate's mind was in a whirl. Could she ever have this man completely? As completely as his love-making? For the moment it didn't matter. That surprised her. She had been raised in the traditional way of saving herself for someone with whom she was in love. But was she in love with this man or the idea of this man? She looked at him dozing quietly by her side.

'What are you thinking Kate?'

'Oh. Only that that was the most satisfying sexual encounter I have ever known.'

'I too, felt the same. Something that I knew would happen. And I am so glad that it did.'

'You mean you have never done this before?' said Kate incredulously.

'No. I wanted it to be with the right woman. A woman I could respect and trust. An honest woman. And you proved that today.' His eyes bored into hers. 'Love should never be taken lightly. You have love in your body and soul. I felt that. It is something to treasure.'

'I felt it too. I never wanted it to end.'

'Then why should it?' he smiled as he took her arms and placed them downwards on the mattress and lifted her back to him in a merging of their bodies that felt the most natural of all.

He eased himself into her slowly and purposefully until he met her fully and clasped her breasts under her body. Whatever had happened before became irrelevant as he brought her to orgasm after orgasm with his rhythmic energy tuned exactly to her own tempo of what heaven must be like. In a final burst of sustained impetus, their world was complete and they collapsed, exhausted onto the bed and slept the sleep of the blessed.

Chapter Forty Nine

Dusk was clinging like a cloak to the overhanging pines as Angus MacManus watched Kate being escorted home by the strange neighbour. There was more than a neighbour in that relationship he noticed. Subtle glances at each other told the observer that they were linked by that inexplicable bond of warmth almost visible between them.

After seeing Kate into Annie's house, the stranger walked back to his cottage. I shall have to deal with him too mused Angus. No one takes my woman. Not even a handsome bastard like you.

He still had in mind catching Kate on her own, but knew that her friend Annie was also in the house. One woman was easy. Two could be risky. He needed a diversion to get Annie away from the house. He snapped his fingers – Andy! That would be the lure.

He retraced his steps through the underbrush to where he had left the car. Another lazy driver who had left his keys dangling in the ignition while he popped into a newspaper shop for the cigarettes that he urgently wanted.

In two seconds Angus was away down the street and into the countryside where his van was hidden under trees forty yards from the main road. Nothing could be seen from the highway, and only a beaten down track, hardly wide enough for a cart, existed to show that anyone had actually driven one down there. Certainly not a car.

The car, a Ford Escort would be ideal for the purpose. It would be reported missing no doubt, but by the time anyone had ordered a search, which did not take priority at the moment, he would have cleared the locality. Lay low for a while until the present tense situation became a little calmer was the safer option. He knew from experience that when an all persons alert was issued, it activated the forces to put all their operational personnel out in the field. When nothing transpired, the forces would be gradually withdrawn as other cases needed attention. When that time came, he would strike.

In the meantime he would soon pay a visit to Andy. Didn't appear to do much work at the bakery, being left behind by his family each morning. That suited Angus.

The sight of Kate walking along with the stranger had jolted him out of his total conviction that Kate still had feelings for him. To see her obviously happy with someone else stirred the rage inside him that threatened to ruin all his plans. He controlled it with difficulty, but it would be held in check until the appropriate moment when the full impact would impel itself onto the subject of his hate.

He couldn't stay in the area for the moment. If he was spotted it would ruin everything. The search parties were covering the district in ever widening circles. He pulled out his road map and traced a route that took him to Glasgow via Loch Ness and Loch Linnhe. From there it was a comparatively short distance to the Lakes. He could hide there for a week or two and then as the clamour died down for his capture, he could return and put his plan into action.

Everyone would be looking for a camper van. That vehicle was gone forever. If his present vehicle was found it would be another diversion for the searchers to scout around that area instead of looking further afield.

Angus drove quietly and within the speed limits, stopping regularly to check for road blocks or patrolling police cars. There were none. The journey took most hours of the night and he eventually pulled into a lay-by for some refreshment. The proprietor of the food bar tried to engage him in social chat, but Angus made his excuses and hid in his car with his tea and bacon sandwich.

Another long day on the road and he saw the signs for Carlisle. He risked a detour around the city and drove deep into the Lake District, his aim, a little inn at the end of a track to Troutbeck.

He had spent his school holidays there with his parents who adored hill walking. A lonely inn with little to do with the more popular tourist areas. No one would look for him there. Sign in under any name and a room was yours for the money up front.

While enjoying a pint of bitter on the bench fronting the inn he reminisced the almost forgotten days of his youth. The gradual rejection by his parents of his wayward attitude to life and the day that he had been cast out of the house to a home for unruly boys. No one believed him about the man who had crept into his bedroom and sexually assaulted him, threatening to kill him if ever he told. He had told, but he was considered to be a willing party and dismissed to the bowels of the awful Borstal like place for "correction."

He spat out the bile that came to his mouth and went to his bed. They would all get their comeuppance when the time came. First on the list was Kate, his beloved betrayer.

Chapter Fifty

'My goodness you are looking in the prime of health this morning Kate.' Annie's remark brought a shy blush to her face.

'I'm feeling good that's why. For once the sun is shining and the worries of the past few weeks have subsided. No one has seen hare or hound of Angus, and his van has at last been found. It was definitely his, as his prints were all over it. Now that he has had to find other transport, perhaps he has had second thoughts and returned to his native haunts where all his friends are.'

'I wouldn't be too sure about that Kate. He's a wily bird from what you've told me. But you're right. We must look on the bright side.' Annie looked quizzically at Kate. 'You're not intending to go back yet though are you?'

'No way. I wouldn't go within a mile of where Angus is. I'll wait it out until he's caught. He'll make a mistake. They all do.' She smoothed her dress over her stomach. Looking guiltily around, she caught Annie watching. 'What?' she exclaimed.

'If I didn't think it was my cooking that was doing you good, I'd say you were pregnant my girl. Always get a bloom in the first month or two.' A large grin split her face. 'Here you haven't been having any hanky panky with Adam have you?'

Kate was nonplussed. She couldn't bring herself to say yes and she couldn't say no. 'What gives you that idea?'

'Always answer a question with another question. That's the best way to avoid being caught out my mum always said.' Annie face relaxed. 'You can tell me you know. I wouldn't blame you if you had.'

Kate felt her tummy. 'It is rather tight. I thought it was all the porridge you've been pushing down me each breakfast. As a matter of fact this is the second month I've missed.' Then as a way of stopping Annie jumping in she said. 'But that is nothing unusual for me. Working shifts and all irregular hours upsets my usual rhythm sometimes.'

'Well as far as I can see, you've experienced another kind of rhythm. One that isn't played on the piano.' Annie burst into laughter and hugged her chum. 'If it's a girl, name it after me will you?'

'Hold on a minute. You're jumping the gun. I haven't seen the doctor yet.'

'So you admit that you are having a tempestuous affair with our handsome neighbour! Shame on you. Didn't even offer to share!'

Kate pushed Annie away. 'You're incorrigible. But now you've mentioned it, we have had our moments and it was absolutely out of this world.' She stopped Annie in her tracks. 'And don't expect me to tell you all the "sordid details" as you would put it.'

'I'm excited Kate. Let's book an appointment to see Doctor Fulton. He's nice. Won't comment on your waywardness or shenanigans. Just give you the verdict. He'll try to offer some advice mind you. He did with me.'

'What! You were pregnant?'

'Thought I was. It was a false alarm. Good job it was. I'd be lumbered with Andy's kid now and what a mess that would have been.' Annie shook her head as she telephoned her doctor.

'Ten a.m. tomorrow. So get your glad rags on and we'll celebrate after the verdict.' She whooped in delight as she danced around Kate simulating a huge stomach with a cushion from the settee. 'We're going to have a baby,' she chortled in song.

Kate sat down and placed her hand in her lap. If it were true, how would she break it to Adam?

Doctor Fulton put away his stethoscope and looked Kate steadily in the eye. A small twitch at the corners of his mouth preceded his announcement. 'It's early days, but I can confirm that you are about seven weeks pregnant. Congratulations.' He did not dwell on whether there was a father present or not. He had seen so many over the past few years to be surprised by any pregnancy. 'A fine healthy woman like you. I don't anticipate any problems.'

That's putting it rather mildly, were Kate's first thoughts. What about the present position she was in? Not married. An ex-husband intent on doing her harm. Lodging with a friend. No idea when she could return to work. What more could go wrong?

'Thank you doctor. What's the procedure now?' Kate was lost. She'd never really discussed motherhood with any of her friends and wouldn't know where to start.

'Here's a handy little booklet that will set you on the right course.' He handed Kate a slim brightly coloured volume that said simply. "Mother and Child."

As she was leaving the surgery, the doctor said. 'On you next appointment I hope I can meet the father.' His smile was genuine.

Kate nodded and hurried into the waiting room to give the news to Annie.

There was an unholy whoop from her friend when Kate confirmed that she was pregnant.

'Ssssh,' said Kate. 'Do you want the whole world to know?'

'Course I do.' Annie whooped again. 'A new life just come into being.' She stopped. 'I take it you're going to tell Adam?'

'I wasn't planning to straight away.'

'If he was your husband, you wouldn't be able to keep it from him for a moment.' Annie saw Kate's face. 'There's nothing wrong is there?'

'No. It's just that .. that... I don't think he's the kind of man .... oh, I don't know. I'm all confused.' Kate was cross with herself for her indecision.

'There's something you're not telling me Kate. Come on; out with it.'

Annie's stern reprimand made Kate try to crystallise her doubts about Adam.

'He's not like other men. He's everything a girl could ever want, but there is a certain reticence in his manner that I haven't been able to get through. I know he's hiding something. Whether on purpose or not, I don't know. He is perfectly honest in everything between us, but there is no background. No stories of his boyhood; of growing up.' Kate turned to her best pal. 'That's not normal is it?'

'I know what you mean. I cannot fault him, but then again, I have nothing to judge him on except the time we have known him.' She set her lips in a stubborn thin line. 'That settles it. You tell him about the baby and then ask him to bring everything out into the open. If you are to be a couple, that is only fair. I don't think he'll refuse.'

A dreadful thought struck Kate. What am I going to do if he does?

'Do you want me to come with you?'

'No I don't! You'd put him off for good. This is a matter between the two of us. Private.' Kate taunted her friend. 'Anyway he'd never reveal anything with you ogling him.'

'True. But if he does reject you, tell him to give me first try will you?' Annie roared with laughter as Kate threw a cushion at her.

Chapter Fifty One

The woman is with child. The gestation period is a little shorter than ours. Generally measured as nine months. As the woman is already over one month into her term, the progeny is expected in the latter part of next year. She is fit and healthy and under the care of the local doctor.

Good. Guard her with your life. Too much has been expended on this undertaking for it to be halted now. Take every precaution necessary. Is there anything we should know?

There is a complication. An evil man is intent on revenge for some past action of the woman. It is believed that he has been in the area and has identified where the woman lives. The police are searching daily but have not been able to apprehend him. She has a gun for protection, but the man is clever. I will keep a vigil day and night.

Trust is the great protector. The trust of the woman must be paramount. Her complete compliance is an essential factor in our future.

Their love is different to ours. It transcends all feelings and is like a heady balm enfolding an invisible umbilical chord to the other person.

It is something that we anticipated. Not that dissimilar from our own. It bodes well.

There is something else. The apostate is once again in Loch Garve. Be prepared for his removal. The soft nosed bullets for your weapon must have the atomic number 72 Hafnium in the nose. Only that will procure the complete termination of the outcast. Two areas are of prime importance. The cerebellum, which controls balance, coordination and posture, is at the base of the brain. The other vital part is the frontal lobe: the controller of behaviour and personality. Both must be destroyed to extinguish this evil.

I have the necessary ammunition. And the ability to carry out what is required.

The ability yes. But ensure that no emotion enters your being at the crucial time. You may have only one chance. We trust in you.

Chapter Fifty Two

Kate answered the telephone's shrill ring. She dreaded the thought that Angus might be on the other end and was guarded in her reply. 'Yes?'

'Kate? This is Detective Inspector Baddeley. We have some news.'

Kate waited anxiously. The tenor of Clare's voice did not give away whether it was good or bad news.

'Angus has been spotted in the Lake District. The description matches that of your friend Annie's – Andy was it? Also the car he was in was reported missing some weeks ago from your district. It was unfortunate that the spotter was a local policeman who could do nothing about it except report it immediately to his superiors. By that time the car had vanished and Angus with it.'

'I suspected that he had moved away from here when he saw the manpower being employed on all roads in and out of the area.'

Clare surmised that Kate had more to add. 'He used to stay in a small inn at Troutbeck - I think it was. You could have a word with them. Sec if he returned to his old haunts.'

'Thanks Kate. But obviously you must be more alert. He will come back now he thinks the search has slackened off. It hasn't you know Kate. It is more undercover now and every police force between the Lakes and Scotland will be on the lookout. Not for the same car, he's too smart for that, but wherever that car turns up will be another link in our pursuit.'

'Have there been any more reports of missing girls?'

'No Kate. Thank goodness. He seems to have put that on the back boiler for the time being. That's why we think that all his concentration will be on finding you.' The Inspector paused. 'You do have a gun don't you Kate?'

'Yes.'

'Keep it loaded. And handy. Do not take any chances with this maniac. I will back you to the hilt should it become necessary …. you know …. police inquests and all that clap trap.'

'Don't worry. We are being watched by a friend of mine. He is aware of the circumstances. Also the local bobby Joe Murray has been a constant caller. Although I sometimes suspect that his other interest is my friend Annie,' laughed Kate.

'Keep plenty of people around you. The local police, and I suppose that includes your Joe Murray, are working round the clock watching the house. In the meantime I'll ring you the moment any concrete sightings have been reported. Good luck Kate.' The Inspector rang off leaving Kate feeling a little depressed that so much attention was necessary. But she knew it was.

She had seen Angus's other side when he was cornered and it wasn't pretty. The vicious way he had killed and disposed of the two girls was abhorrent. Scenes that the public had never seen and never would, remained etched deeply in her memory. Which reminded her that the second girl reported missing locally had still not been found. Where had he disposed of her? If Angus was responsible.

Kate decided to give Adam a visit to bring him up to date. There was a lot to discuss about the baby and the future. He had not indicated that he had any intentions toward marriage, but the joy he had shown had more than compensated for the time being. It had been a shock to Kate, but the impression she got from Adam was that the pregnancy was as natural as if he had fully expected to become a father. Another strange phenomenon that worried her. His lack of understanding of the vagaries of two people actually hitting the jackpot first time. Kate smiled at her own thoughts on what was an apt comparison.

Annie came in from the kitchen to disturb her thoughts. 'A penny for them Kate. What is the most important item that you should be thinking about?'

'The baby of course. What else?'

'You're right. From now on he, or she, is number one.'

'Oh didn't I tell you? It is a boy.' Kate's face betrayed nothing.

'How do you know? Have you got a crystal ball?' Then she saw the triumphant look in Kate's eye.

'Adam! He's told you it is a boy, right? The fathers all say that.' She scoffed at Kate's satisfied grin. 'Cause deep inside they all want a boy. Stands to reason doesn't it? Carry on the line.'

'Yes. Adam did say it is a boy. Not that he hopes it is a boy. But quite categorically – a boy.'

'And you believed him? What does the doctor say? "You'll have to wait" I bet.'

'He hasn't said anything, only that it is healthy and coming along fine. I feel well, no morning sickness, a little ache in my back now and again, but apart from that I'm OK.'

'Anything else worrying you?' Annie had noticed the uncertainty hidden behind the apparent bonhomie.

'Clare Baddeley has been on the phone. Angus has been spotted in the Lake District.'

'That's good isn't it? As far away from here as possible.'

'But she thinks that he may be on his way back.' Kate bit her lip. 'To find me she says. He mustn't know I'm pregnant. It will tip him over the edge.'

'How do you mean?'

'After we had been married for two years and trying for a baby I persuaded him, or rather I told him, we should both be tested to see whether there was any reason why we were not compatible. He refused at first, blaming it all on me. Finally after I was confirmed as OK, he went along. He was told that he could never have children. It shattered him.'

'Do you think that was what pushed him over the edge?'

'Probably. But there must have been something there already to turn his mind to ..... what he did.'

Annie made a cup of tea and they sat and consoled each other that they were well protected and that it was likely that the police would trace him if he made his way north again.

Kate was not so sure. She put on her heavy coat and told Annie that she was off to see Adam.

'Not on your own you're not!' exclaimed Annie.

'Don't be silly. It's only two hundred yards or so. And in any case, there is a patrol car that regularly passes and the police have a round the clock watch on. Angus will spot that a mile off, so even Angus will realise that he can't beat it.'

As Kate walked along the road, she was not as sure that her logic was infallible, but her spirits were boosted a little when the patrol car dogged her footsteps all the way to Adam's.

Three people, perched on the heights were watching the scene below them. Two plain clothes officers and one other.

Angus MacManus smiled as he noted the position of the police and the patrol car. He took into account the geography of the land between the two houses. A plan began to develop in his fertile mind.

Chapter Fifty Three

The ever present pungent smell of manure was everywhere. It was ingrained in every farmer's clothes and lumps of it clung to their boots. Cows moaned over the sounds of bleating and squawking, with pigs screaming every time they were kicked into the auction ring. Over the babble of the auctioneer declaiming the value of each batch that came under his hammer there was a general buzz of farm matters and jocularity among the onlookers.

Tweeds, hats, pipes, and sticks were the order of the day. Larger than life bloated faces pushed their reddened noses into every transaction that took their fancy. Angular women elbowed their way to the front, most with ample bosoms and backsides to match. Their men meanwhile took a well earned breather in the adjacent "Farmers' Arms" on the edge of the cattle market.

Beer flowed as quickly as the constant urine being despatched by the uneasy cows. Rings of froth splattered the bar top, to be mopped up by unobservant farmers propping themselves into a static position in case they should succumb to the alcohol's effect.

The noise inside was more than a pen full of sheep could compete with. Prices, quality, the batch bought only a month ago, milk yields and fat content – all were bandied about as if it were a competition to see who could tell the tallest tale.

In the corner, one farmer sat drooling over his beer. Tightly bunched between others, he rarely partook in any interplay between the laughing landowners. His mind was set on the gaping door.

He didn't have long to wait. The light was blocked for a moment as PC Joe Murray strode over to the bar and greeted mine host with 'The usual please landlord.' The landlord duly obliged with a frothy topped dark ale brimming over the rim of the thick tankard.

'Ta very much Alf. Anything to report?' PC Joe Murray's words were echoed every market day as he sought to ferret out any unusual activity around the market. A lot of smuggling was abroad at this time of year and the constable would love to nip it in the bud.

'No. You could book this crowd into the bar every week. Never change. No one here that I know of doing anything underhand.' He changed tack. 'Where's that mate of yours? Never bring him in here.'

'He's teetotal. Prefers to keep an eye on what's going on outside. Good though.' Then Joe said rather proudly. 'We're on patrol together tomorrow, along the Loch Garve road. Looking forward to that.'

The landlord carried on serving, washing glasses, and talking at the same time. He had failed to notice the strange farmer in the corner though. Roughly dressed in cord trousers and dark check jacket with an open shirt and a muffler topped with a well worn cap; he was not one of the regulars.

Angus MacManus took careful note of Joe Murray. A thirty year old, passed over for promotion, but a solid constable nevertheless. Called in the bar without fail every Friday market day. Regular as clockwork. Always left his partner outside. That's where they fall down, smiled Angus.

You can set your clock by them. Make an entry in a diary and it will be fulfilled.

Downing his pint, the constable walked slowly out of the pub. No one paid him any notice. Except Angus. Slipping away from the crush of the farmers on either side of him he followed Joe Murray out of the door. The gap on the bench where he had been sitting, closed as if he had never existed.

Joe picked up his partner and drove the police Land Rover slowly out of the town into a suburban area mostly filled with cheap housing and prefabs. Joe Murray lived in a corner terraced house, two up and two down. Living on his own for over ten years since his parents died, he was self sufficient and maintained a smart home with good neighbours.

He parked his car outside his house and entered through the well varnished door. His colleague remained in the vehicle. Angus observed the scene from the end of the street. After about ten minutes Joe emerged again and made for the police station to make his report. He had not been requisitioned for the priority job of searching for Angus MacManus. That irked him. Just because he had remained an ordinary constable didn't mean he couldn't do a specialist job. All they had given him was a patrol along the road fronting Loch Garve.

His thoughts were on the frustration of not being part of a "team" as he pulled into the yard, dropped the other constable off, and entered the station to make his report on his shift.

Angus knew the routine and fully expected Joe to clock off for the evening. He was proved correct when Joe drove home and parked for the night in the side street abutting his house.

Angus calculated that Joe Murray and one other were on the 4pm shift if nothing untoward cropped up. That suited Angus. The nights were dark and any time after 4pm was ideal for his purpose.

He made his way back to the quiet spot in the forest fringing the loch to await his appointment with Joe the following evening. But before that he had another appointment with Andy McBride, who didn't know it but he was the key to the chain of events that would lead to Angus exacting the revenge and punishment he had promised himself every day he had spent in that hell hole of a prison in Manchester.

No one, but no one, ever got the better of Angus MacManus.

Chapter Fifty Four

Saturday morning was hectic. Annie and Kate had a mountain of goods to load into the van and drive to the market town to set up their stall.

'You needn't come if you don't feel up to it Kate.' Annie turned as Kate carried a box of crockery from the house.

'I'm OK. The exercise will do me good. I've got over my morning sickness and the fresh air will put new strength in my limbs.' Kate breathed hard after depositing the load.

'You don't fool me my darling. You're all but knackered if you all but knew it. Pregnancy isn't a bed of roses. It's nine months hard work and you've only just started.'

'Others seem to cope.'

'Seem is the operative word. Nobody ever sees them at home when they lay exhausted on the couch, unable to sit upright.' Annie took another box from Kate. 'At least let me do all the humping will you. You've done enough.'

They both caught on to the reference at the same time and burst into laughter. 'At least I've something to show for my humping.'

The van loaded, they set off for the town in good spirits.

Their journey was again observed by the three onlookers. The presence of one of whom would have scared the daylights out of them.

Angus ran through his timetable. Back about four o'clock. Joe returns home about four fifteen. Andy is always in the house at tea-time. Perfect.

The police are fools. I've been back in the district for over a week now, and no one has come anywhere near my hideout. Angus congratulated himself on his cleverness. He had disposed of the car the police were looking for – that is if they had followed the trail of exchanges since the Lakes. On foot now and living in an abandoned hut deep in the forest, inaccessible to all but the most competent of foresters. He had learnt his trade with the army before entering the police on discharge. He swore under his breath as he remembered being dismissed early "due to unsuitability for his rank."

No one had ever been able to prove it, but young girls on the camp had been approached by a man in a balaclava and assaulted. Suspicion was rife throughout the camp and several men were suspected. The Colonel had decided on drastic action. "If you can't identify the root source, get rid of the scourge." All those under suspicion and unable to prove their innocence were thrown out on grounds of unsuitability. Angus was one of them. That way the camp was "clean" once again. Fully justified by the immediate cessation of any similar activity happening subsequently.

Angus had mapped out a route to Andy's place. The bicycle he intended to use would belay any suspicion in the area. The forecast for the following day was heavy rain and thunderstorms. Again perfect. Nothing like rain and overcast skies to disguise a person. The so called surveillance by the police using their rain spattered binoculars could be deceived by appearances. And Angus was very good at that.

The haversack was packed. Everything he would need. The Walther PPK with silencer tucked into the pocket of the sack. The knife housed in a special scabbard to go around his waist. The key to the outboard motor safely tucked away in his pocket. That had been the risky part. Killing the sole owner of the loch side bungalow, hiding his body, and purloining his key to the dinghy tied to the quay at the bottom of his garden.

People are so careless, he chortled, recalling the look of surprise on the man's face as he thrust the knife up and into the fatal area of his heart. That's the last trip you'll take my friend, he whispered as he returned the body to the water's edge and sank it with a large stone.

The dingy was now moored within easy distance of his hideaway. Ready for tomorrow.

Chapter Fifty Five

Adam settled down on his waterproof blanket, legs spread wide apart and perfectly still. The 7.62 Winchester rifle stretched out in front of him on its special tripod, was an extension of his body. From his high position on a promontory, he aligned the sighting on the far end of the lake, adjusting for each range from 100 yards to 400 yards. Capable of much more than that distance, it could be deadly accurate in the right hands.

The water was still as a millpond. Unusual for this time of year, as the trees bent unsuccessfully to shield themselves from the bitter cold. The forests edging the loch on both sides were showing their woody strength as the canopy of green thinned. Water birds were in a minority, most having flown off to winter in South Africa as the conditions became arctic on the Scottish Highlands.

The cold did not worry Adam. His skin shone with a sheen that appeared to mirror the water around him. His strong, slender fingers cushioned the rifle against any movement induced by his breathing. He knew he could hit any target within the range of the rifle.

He was waiting for that target.

His thoughts wandered to Kate and the baby she was expecting and he was confused by the inner pride and buoyancy that the news had given him. His senses had been changed over the past few weeks and it puzzled him that the range of emotions within him now felt part of his inner ego. He gloried in the fact that it gave him purpose and an anchor to the life he now lived.

His eyes caught a movement on the west side of the loch. A disturbance in the water as the ripples skipped silently away from the shore to die in the far reaches of the depths. The cause of the ripples appeared soon after. A dinghy was gliding over the surface close in to the shore with a solitary occupant. Not venturing into the deeper part of the loch, the dinghy clung to the overhanging trees until it found its berth. A little inlet hidden from view of anyone walking the footpaths.

Curious was Adam's first thought. Whoever it was had some purpose in mind that did not tally with normal behaviour. There was nothing in that spot. Adam had passed it many times on his runs. There was no hunting around there and certainly no fishing.

He kept watch for another three and a half hours until dusk, waiting for the dingy to emerge. There was no further disruption of the slate smooth loch to indicate an intruder on its preserve.

Adam picked up the Winchester and stowed the gun in its waterproof holder. Picking up the tripod, he slid down the small incline to reach the rough track battered down by his feet each morning. His smooth and efficient loping stride took him to where he had seen the dinghy last.

A quick search and he found it. It had been half pulled up on to the shore and tied to a tree branch with its twin screw outboard motor tipped at an angle over the rear. Adam looked round for the owner. Nothing showed in the nearby trees to say that he was in the vicinity.

Something worried Adam about the find. At the moment there was no logical explanation nor was there any reason to believe that it was anything else but an innocent excursion by the owner. Wherever and whoever he is.

Adam would maintain his vigil over the loch the next day. He did not want the dingy to be a distraction from the assignment that was paramount in his thoughts.

Chapter Fifty Six

'Who's there?' Andy shouted down the long hallway. There was no reply.

'I said who's there?' The knocking continued.

'Bloody hell. Can't you understand soddin' English?' He wrenched open the door and froze.

'Hello Andy. Can I come in?' Angus MacManus flashed his ID momentarily and strode past the startled ex-husband of Annie before he could respond.

'What are you doing here again? I thought we'd finished our business last time.'

Angus smiled. 'Well you thought wrong didn't you? That's the trouble with scum like you Andy. You don't think.' He helped himself to the whisky on the sideboard. 'Good malt this. Is it your dad's?'

'Bugger off will you. You've nothing on me. Otherwise you would have taken me in last time.' Andy's leer now overcame the initial fear of being confronted with the law.

'I want you to do a little favour for me Andy,' said Angus smoothly.

'A favour!? You must be bleedin' mad! Since when have I done any favours for the filth?'

Angus slowly drew his Walther PPK from the back of his trousers. 'I think you will cooperate now, won't you Andy?'

'Geez! Put that thing away! It might go off!'

'More than likely. That is if you don't do as you're told.' Angus's manner changed to one of cold menace. 'Get your coat.'

Andy didn't need telling twice. He could see the hard glint now replacing the previous sociable light in Angus's eyes and rushed to the hall stand.

'Into the car. And drive. You can drive can't you?' Angus thrust Andy into the driving seat from the passenger side, keeping the gun trained on him the whole time.

Andy didn't reply.

'Go to the main road and take a right turn.'

Andy did as he was told.

'How's your grandmother Andy?' The question disoriented Andy for a moment as he wondered what the hell was going on.

'How did you know about her?'

'I do my research. Ninety one isn't she? Tucked up in that Grosvenor Nursing Home, near the sea. Must cost a packet. But still, your family can afford it. All those cakes and bread. Given you a good living hasn't it. Not that you've done a stroke to benefit from it.' Angus dug the gun into Andy's left side. 'Stop here.'

The car pulled up onto the verge as Angus yanked Andy over the central shaft housing and out of the passenger door.

Angus's glare now matched the darkening red of the surrounding brush. He roughly shoved Andy toward the red telephone box that was the only sign of civilisation for miles around.

'Dial Annie. Tell her that your granny's ill. Dying. Wants to see her before she goes. Very fond of Annie wasn't she? One of her favourites. Annie liked her too didn't she?'

'I can't do that. She'll never believe me.'

Angus rammed the gun into the side of his head. 'Perhaps this will encourage you to make it good. If not ….'

'OK! OK! Just give me a minute!'

'Don't forget. Your granny wants to see her straight away. It's very important.' Again Andy felt the cold barrel of the silencer against his cheek.

'Annie? Look! Don't ring off. I've something very urgent to tell you.' Andy took a breath and blurted out the story of his nan's illness and urged her to come immediately to the Grosvenor Nursing Home.' He almost shouted down the phone. 'Don't worry; I won't be there. I've just come from there.'

'Good Andy. That was very convincing,' Angus said. He had heard Annie gasp and say that she would come as soon as possible and that she hoped she would be in time.

'You were quite right you know,' Andy said casually as he replaced the receiver. 'You won't be there.'

He shot Andy in the back of the head and calmly left the telephone box, smiling to himself as the door swung back on Andy's iron coffin.

Chapter Fifty Seven

'Got to go out Kate. Andy's granny is seriously ill and wants to see me. You'll be OK won't you? There's plain clothes police watching and a patrol car every hour or so. Don't go out. Lock all the doors when I've gone and don't open them to anyone.'

'Stop all the fuss. I'm quite capable of looking after myself you know. Now get along before the light gets too bad. And drive carefully.'

'Hark who's making a fuss now! See you as soon as I can. I'll ring you with an update and when I am likely to be back.' Annie donned her heavy coat and put on her beret and scarf and was gone.

Should I go to see Adam? thought Kate. Would the police object to my going out? Better not. It was getting dark and it would be difficult to see if anything suspicious was happening around the cottage.

The baby was growing. She could actually see a slight swelling now.

Kate had been delighted with the reaction from Adam. For a time she had thought that he would be non committal, but he was so attentive whenever they met that her feelings for him deepened more than she had hoped. How is it that I have slept with a man who I had barely known for more than a few weeks and yet I feel so uplifted?

Adam too had shown the kind of compassion for which she thought he was incapable. From the rather stiff, withdrawn and sombre character that had first confronted her and Annie, he had become … what was the word she was seeking? More human.

She gasped at her phrase. Why should she have thought that he was not human? Admittedly there were times when she had apprehended someone and described them to her colleagues as "inhuman" but that was different.

Angus was inhuman. Anyone who could carry out the bestial attacks on poor little girls as he had, deserved to be called inhuman. That was the word that the judge had used and Kate had applauded him quietly from the back of the court.

When they eventually found the girls, their clothing was missing and it was confirmed that both had been sexually assaulted many times, and then their throats were cut as if they were pigs at an abattoir.

Kate shook her head to rid herself of the images.

There was a noise from the kitchen. She panicked and picked up the steel poker before going to investigate. It was the kettle coming to the boil. She had switched it on as Annie left. Nothing like a cup of tea to calm the nerves. And a gun.

She fetched the rifle from its store in the hall cupboard and ensured that it was loaded. She propped it up against the old stone fireplace.

The best feature about a gun, she thought, is if you never have to use it.

There came a knock on the door. She looked through the spyhole that had been inserted when the alert was first raised. It was one of the observers, known to Kate.

'Hello,' she said.

'Hi. Just to let you know that we are changing shifts now and the new blokes will be coming on duty. You know them. They are already in position. Goodnight.'

'Goodnight. And thank you.' Kate closed the door and sat by the fire.

If you're out there Angus, I hope you are freezing your balls off. Annie would have laughed at that chuckled Kate.

Chapter Fifty Eight

Joe Murray finished his ham sandwich, savouring the liberal amount of mustard he had daubed on and climbed into the Police Land Rover. His partner for the evening was Frank Rogers, a forty year old regular constable, content with his lot. Small for a policeman at five foot nine inches, he had more than made up for his lack of height by his ability to talk down people.

A true Scotsman and patriot, he would have nothing to do with anyone who wasn't. Few dared to challenge him. His ginger hair sat neatly under his cap drawn down to just above his eyebrows causing a horizontal line across his red speckled face. Green eyes went with the hair and he was secretly known as "Ginger Rogers."

'Hi Frank,' Joe said as he propelled himself into the driver's seat via the step. Frank did not answer. Joe nudged him and Frank fell sideways onto the side window.

'Christ Frank, whatever happened to you?' Then Joe saw the neat hole in the back of Frank's head and the gaping exit wound over the top of his eyes.

'This did sunshine. And it will happen to you if you don't do as you're told.' Angus thrust the gun barrel into the back of Joe's neck from the rear seat.

Joe froze. He didn't need to turn round to scc who it was.

'Drive.' The one word command jolted Joe into movement. 'And if you try anything funny, that's the last laugh you'll ever have.'

Joe started the engine. 'Which way?' He desperately searched for something to distract the murderer behind him.

'I'll tell you when to turn. And keep your eyes on the road. If anyone stops us, remember I will shoot them first then you.'

Joe could tell by the tenor of the voice that the man was hyped up. A kind of unnatural, off key timbre that heightened his nervous state.

At the main road he was told to turn right and drive at normal speed. After a few hundred yards when the Land Rover had cleared the town, he was ordered to stop.

The passenger door opened from the inside and Frank was pushed out into the bracken at the road edge. He rolled over twice and then was still.

Angus leaned over and hauled the door shut, climbing over the seat to threaten Joe with his all too prominent gun. 'Carry on then,' he said, as if he was on a conducted tour. Joe noticed the police uniform and Frank's borrowed hat which now sat on Angus MacManus's head.

Three miles down the road Joe's fears came true. They were on the road that took them past Annie's house. He had called regularly to re-assure Kate Grainger that there had been no sign of Angus MacManus. What could he tell her this time? If he was allowed to.

'Pull over to the hard shoulder next to the gate. That's what you usually do isn't it? Act normally and no one will get hurt. Try anything and you get it first.' Joe did not doubt for one minute that the threat would be carried out. All he could do was to go along with it, hoping that an opportunity would arise when he could go for Angus.

‘Knock on the door.’ Another command that Joe thought about disobeying. If he did, it would only delay Angus from forcing the door open, leaving the women with nobody to try to help them.

He rapped in his usual manner. He waited until he was identified through the spyhole.

The door opened. Kate stood there. ‘Hello Joe,’ she said. ‘Annie has been called away.’

For one moment Joe thanked god that she had been, then realised it was selfish of him. There was still the menace of the man behind him.

‘What is it Joe? You look dreadful.’

Angus stepped out from behind Joe. ‘Get your coat Kate. You’re going for a ride.’

Kate gasped and was about to scream when Angus stepped close and almost thrust the gun down Joe’s throat. ‘One noise and Joe gets it now!’

Kate stifled the yell which came out like a half strangled chicken’s croak.

‘Inside Joe. I said get your coat Kate. And make it quick.’ He menaced them with the gun and explained that they were going to walk steadily to the car; Joe in front with Kate behind at the side of Angus. Everything must look like a normal pick up, he emphasized. He would put a bullet in the first one to raise any alarm.

The police observers would be watching and she knew Angus’s intention was that it should look quite normal. “Taking Kate to the station for her own protection” would be the inference. What could she do to tip off the watchers without Angus being aware of it?

She had her answer in the shape of the hard metal rammed up into her ribs under cover of Angus’s arm guiding her to the car. She could not afford to risk Joe’s life by being a hero, even if she could.

Joe climbed into the driver’s seat and Angus helped Kate into the rear. He joined her and told Joe to drive off. Slowly.

As the Land Rover pulled away from the cottage, the two watchers conferred with each other and decided that matters had reached the stage where Kate's presence in the house could not be completely protected. Joe Murray and his partner had Kate under their charge and she would be safe for the time being. Recent conferences in the squad room had confirmed that Angus MacManus was in the area. Stolen cars and brief unsubstantiated sightings were enough to alert the squad that he was running out of time. That meant that the police tactics had to change to meet any contingency. Get Kate to a safe haven was the important factor.

The two watchers came down from their high vantage point and made their way to the car parked out of sight in the forest nearby.

'What are you doing Angus?' Kate decided to engage her former husband and keep him talking. That way she might be able to calm him down and discover what his plans were.

'I am renewing our association Kate. We have lost a lot of time over the past few months and we need to make up for it.'

'Let Joe go. You don't want him. You have what you want. Me.'

'Very gallant of you Kate. Always knew you were a plucky lass. But it won't do. I need poor old Joe for the moment.' He relapsed into a silent grimace.

'The police will soon pick up your trail. They've been expecting you.' It was a futile attempt to unnerve him Kate thought.

'Not soon enough. A patrol car calls at the house, picks up the occupant and drives away to somewhere safe. This Land Rover is not due to return to the station for some time. Right Joe? By that time we shall be far away.' His gloating voice ground into Kate's mind as she realised that he was right. Everything would appear normal until the watchers arrived at the station for their report.

'What made you come to Scotland Kate? Was it a yearning for my home country?' Angus leered into her face. 'Found a new boyfriend haven't you?

Kate blanched. What did he know of Adam? How long had he been watching them? 'We have a friend, yes.' Kate emphasised the "we."

'No Kate. You have a friend. Annie has her own friend. That right Joe?' He dug Joe in the neck with his gun.

'Yes … er … yes. Annie and I are friends.' Joe tried to keep calm as he desperately searched for an escape plan. When they stopped, he decided. Angus could only cover one at a time, and when he was concentrating on Kate he would charge him.

'So we have two pairs of little lovebirds. How sweet.' Angus was enjoying himself. Everything was going to plan.

Kate and Joe kept quiet. Angus peered out of the windscreen as the road, now running with a sudden downpour, became less distinct. 'Put your wipers on full Joe! Can't see a thing!'

'They are on full. It's dangerous to drive in this sort of weather. It comes down from the mountains on our right. There could be landfalls or a piece of the road swept away.'

'Then we'll just have to risk it won't we?' Angus's scornful voice competed with the violent hammering of the rain on the roof. 'Afraid to die are we Joe?'

'I'm not afraid, but I'm not so silly as to take unnecessary risks. You'll kill us all.'

'You could be right there Joe. That would be a pity before I've got what I came for.'

Kate let the shattering noise of the storm ease a little before she said. 'Look Angus. If you turn yourself in now, I am sure that in the circumstances it will better for you. This way can only end in tragedy.'

'You're right again Kate. But whose tragedy are you talking about? You forget that I am a policeman. We were all taught to reason with a gunman. Did any of it work for you in the past? No, course it didn't.' His laugh was getting more and more delirious as Kate sensed that his mind had deteriorated to the point of insanity the judge had quoted in his summing up.

'Stop here!' Angus waved the gun at the two of them. 'Climb out. I'm watching you both very carefully.'

Joe got out of the cab and opened the rear door for Kate. He helped her onto the pine needle strewn ground and stood helplessly as Angus climbed down to join them. He was careful to keep both in his sights as he motioned them to walk into the trees thickly bunched on either side of the narrow path.

Within ten minutes they were free of the dark overhanging branches and emerging into the pale moonlight of the wintery backdrop of the ripple-edged shimmering water of Loch Garve.

'Into the boat!' He motioned to Joe. 'You drive! Remember I shall have the gun against Kate's body the whole way.' As if to emphasise his point he gave Kate a painful jab in the ribs. She gasped with pain. 'That's it my beauty. Enjoy the ride while you can. Treat it as a cruise to paradise.'

Chapter Fifty Nine

Adam peered as the storm whipped up the surrounds of Loch Garve. Dark and dreary as a funeral procession, it fought to hide its secrets from the outside world.

Adam knew what lurked beneath and was waiting for his opportunity. His Winchester at the ready.

Something disturbed his vigilance. A movement on the water. The sound of an outboard motor dulled by the storm, but tugging at his senses. Soon he spotted the boat on the right hand side of where he had set up his watch.

His eyes accustomed to the gloom, discerning three people, two at the prow and one on the engine.

Kate! he almost cried out. And Joe in the rear with a man almost cuddling his beloved in the prow. Angus! Somehow he had captured them and was taking them to the other side of the loch. Could he risk a shot? Too dangerous. Angus's body was covered by Kate's, probably with a gun in her ribs.

Adam shot out of his hide and raced down to the loch shore and shouldering his rifle protected by a waterproof cover, he dived into the now foaming water. With strong strokes he strove to keep up with the progress of the boat across the loch but the pace was impossible.

He needed a spot where he could watch the three when they disembarked. There he could assess the situation and make his move. He knew of a clearing on the other side, a hundred or so yards from the water's edge where the boat appeared to he heading.

Clambering up the stony bank he made for a high vantage point overlooking the spot where he anticipated the three would have made for. He was right. Angus and Kate and Joe were in the clearing. Kate was being tied to a tree by Joe. Angus threatened them both with his gun and then waved Joe to the side where an ominous spade was thrust into the ground. Joe started digging.

He plans to kill them and then bury them was the obvious thought thudding in Adam's brain.

Carefully unsheathing his rifle, Adam focused on the figure of Angus. Still shielded by the circle of trees, he waited his chance for a clean shot. He must not miss. As he gauged the wind and the distance and the trajectory of the bullet, his gaze remained icy calm and his hands steady.

Suddenly something made Angus scream out loud. Joe was running for the boat, scrambling and desperately pulling the starting rope. The sound as it burst into life echoed over the loch like a triumphant blast of freedom.

Angus, now recovered from whatever had spiked him, charged down to the shore after Joe. Leaning on a tree trunk, he held the gun in a double grip and fired two shots. Joe fell poleaxed into the boat. The second shot took out the engine and the boat was marooned on the dark alien waters.

Adam considered his options. The head shot was favourite. Instant death. He waited for the killer to return to the circle where he would be visible for a decisive shot. Angus stood menacingly over Kate mocking her.

Adam re-sighted and settled into his rock steady stance. As his finger moved imperceptibly against the tension of the trigger, his sights were marred by an object moving slowly into his view. A familiar black shape stood between him and his target.

Adam relaxed his grip and watched.

A grim smile played across his perfectly formed lips. Two evils in one place at the same time. Save Kate first. His other mission could wait.

Chapter Sixty

'Tie her up tight. I'll check when you've done.' Angus shouted at Joe as he wound the rope around Kate's body, now sitting hunched against a tree trunk.

'Brace your arms and your wrists as much as you can,' whispered Joe as he pretended to pull the ropes taut. 'I'll try and surprise him.'

'Hurry up.' Angus strode across the clearing waving Joe away as he checked the binding.

'Now get digging. Wide enough for two.'

Joe reluctantly picked up the spade and scraped the carpet of needles and cones from the ground. The surface was hard and he smashed the spade in and found only roots blocking his progress. 'There's too many roots,' he shouted.

'Then dig round them.' Angus came across to look at what was only a scrape in the hard ground. 'Try over here then.'

Joe swung his spade into the new ground and found soft earth. Taking a shovel full he swung in an arc and peppered Angus with a shower of shale and rubble, knocking him off his feet and blinding him for a second. The gun shot out of his grasp and Joe made a dive for it at the same time as Angus. He lost. He pushed Angus into the bracken and turned to Kate.

'Go Joe, go!' screamed Kate. 'Get help!' Joe took off as fast as he could for the shore of the loch. Angus roared as he scrambled to regain his feet. 'You won't get far you bastard!'

He charged after Joe, gun in hand, eyes blazing. As he passed Kate she shot out her left leg in a horizontal kick with her hard shoes pointing at his knee. She caught him full on the kneecap with all the force she could muster.

Angus went down screaming in agony and clutching his leg. 'You little whore,' he swore. 'You'll pay for that.'

Kate desperately tried to loosen her bonds more. What little freedom she had gained had enabled her to launch herself at Angus with a full blooded kick. That gave her some satisfaction and also a slim chance for Joe to escape.

Angus was up and ignoring the pain, scrambled down to the loch shore. Standing against a nearby tree he adopted a two handed grip of the gun as he had been taught in the police training school, and took precise aim.

The first shot hit Joe, tipping him forward into the boat. The second shot killed the engine and the dinghy drifted helplessly in the middle of the loch.

Kate watched in horror as Angus returned. 'Now we'll tie you up again. This time there will be no leeway.'

He wound the rope around Kate knotting it viciously into her wrists. As he completed the truss, his hand passed across her stomach and Kate nearly wretched.

'Oh oh …. What have we here then?' He smoothed his hand round and over the curve as she sat unable to move. 'Who's been playing away then?'

Kate sat numb. She was wrestling with how she should approach the situation. Must think straight, she reminded herself. How many times had she been up against criminals and what were the procedures for dealing with the insane? For that was what Angus was now. Completely wrapped up in his quest, whatever that was. Keep his mind occupied was at the forefront of her tactics. Talk to him as if he were still her husband.

She laughed at his joke. 'You must be confused. I've just put a little weight on that's all. It's the way of life up here.' She stared straight into those deranged eyes that now echoed the destruction of any logical thoughts he may have had.

'Don't fool me Kate. I know a pregnancy when I see one. We tried long enough didn't we? But it was me wasn't it?' he screamed, tormenting himself more and more as he ranted about his impotency.

'You wouldn't admit it would you?' chided Kate. Determined now to keep him talking at all costs. He was going to kill her, there was no doubt about that. But she would fight to the end, hoping that help would somehow come.

'Is that why you turned to little girls? They couldn't know you were not a full man could they?' Kate trembled as she saw his face twist in a snarl and he hit her across her mouth.

'They never complained like you did, you bitch!' He took out his knife from the leather sheath on his belt. 'Now, how far are you gone? Not too far I hope.' His insane grin took on the semblance of a rabid dog with spittle oozing from his blue lips. 'What were you hoping to get Kate? A boy or a girl?'

Kate felt herself loosing her grip. She drew her legs underneath her as far as possible and shouted at him. 'You could have had children if you'd only sought help. There are many ways of overcoming a deficiency such as yours.' She almost laughed. Here she was in fear of her life, discussing fertility with her ex-husband! But he was still talking.

Kate continued. 'What did you do with the little girl from up here? Another one of your conquests. You must be very brave, despoiling a weak child who cannot fight back. You're a fraud.'

'No! They are all tramps! They taunt me because they know! They have to die!' His hands went to his head and tried to stop the images appearing to leer at him. 'You're a tramp too. Look at you. Only up here for a few short weeks and you get yourself up the spout.' He was raging now, unable to comprehend anything that Kate threw at him.

He looked down at his knife. Then reality set in. 'Yes … that's it … don't know what sex it is do we?.... then we'll find out. You'll see your bastard child a lot sooner than you thought.' His maniacal laugh screamed its triumph through the trees. Then there was silence.

Angus stopped. There was no sound. Kate had stopped whimpering. The trees stopped rustling. Utter darkness and quiet filled the circle like a black hole blocking out all senses.

Angus cocked is head. There was a sound he didn't recognise immediately behind him. He froze. Then pulling his gun he swung round and gasped.

He was looking straight into the luminous eyes of a large black horse. It stood there motionless. Just staring. Angus's crazy mind went berserk. He dropped his gun and tried to run but couldn't. He was rooted to the spot.

The horse stepped forward, lowered its head and grasped Angus's coat in its teeth. With one ferocious snap of its neck, it swung Angus up and over onto its back.

Kate sat aghast. She saw the translucent sheen of the horse's coat and its proud stance. There was something in its eyes that she couldn't quite identify, something familiar. It stood for a moment, locked in a gaze at Kate. Then it bared its teeth and a cry from hell blasted out of its mouth. Leaping like a cat pouncing on a mouse, it shot off at a gallop along the shore with a terrified Angus howling in the night.

Chapter Sixty One

Kate was distraught. Joe dead. Her ex-husband about to die. The violation of her body and the realisation that she was about to be mutilated, all crushed in on her mind until she collapsed in a mangled heap against the restraints of the ropes binding her. Her sobs came in great gasps as she fought to make sense of the last few minutes.

She felt a hand on her shoulder.

'Ahhh!!' she screamed and scrabbled her feet against the forest floor in an effort to shy away from whatever was threatening her.

'Shush my darling,' a voice whispered in her ear. 'Everything is going to be all right.' She felt her bindings loosen and soon she was free. She looked up and saw Adam, who took her in his arms and held her tight. 'I just want a minute then I'll be back.'

She watched as Adam turned and easily unsheathed his rifle from the carrier on his back. He dropped to one knee and levelled it at the loch.

Kate was now able to see the horse with a raving Angus on its back, swimming steadily toward the centre of the loch. Adam was rock steady. His rifle like a projection of his body. He took aim and two shots rang out. The intensity of the noise rocked Kate on her heels as she saw the horse rear up out of the water and crash down like a whale in the surf. Angus went with it and both were out of sight within seconds.

Adam re-sheathed his rifle and took hold of Kate. 'You're safe now. Nothing can harm you.'

'What about Angus? What has happened to him? I don't understand.'

Adam looked into Kate's wild eyes. He slowly nodded and turned. His rifle was discarded and he ran deer-like along the shore until he was level with where the horse and rider had gone down. He dived in. Kate gasped. She couldn't believe what was happening. 'Adam!' she cried. But it was lost in the wind.

She stood anxiously staring at the unforgiving water. Nothing moved. It was as if the world was standing still again. Then a head broke the surface. Adam's! And then another floating helplessly behind Adam.

The two managed to get to the shore where Adam dragged Angus to where Kate stood spellbound.

'He's still alive,' said Adam. 'Doesn't deserve to be.'

'I know, but he is insane. In the end he had no control over what he was doing. Oh God! I can't believe it.' She threw herself into Adam's arms and sobbed.

'I have to go Kate. The police will be here soon. They have found the body of the policeman. Joe isn't dead. He reached the other shore and radioed for help.'

Adam searched around until he found a thick branch. 'Here. Tie Angus up with the rope. We don't want him to come round do we?' He then took the branch and hit Angus over the head with a sharp blow. 'Not enough to do any damage, but enough to convince the police of your story.'

'My story?'

'You escaped from your binding and hit him over the head and then tied him up.'

'Why do I have to say that?'

'Because, my love, I would have too many awkward questions to answer if I am found here.' Adam kissed her full on the lips and walked away from her to the loch as the sound of a motorcade filtered through the trees and lights began searching for Kate.

'See you back on the other side,' Adam whispered loud enough for Kate to hear.

Kate smiled for the first time that evening. She felt a warmth inside and a growing sense of fulfilment. Her Adam.

But why had he shot the horse?

Chapter Sixty Two

Joe Murray slowly opened his eyes. He searched for something familiar, but could not recognise his surroundings. His sense of smell gave him a clue. A hospital. What am I doing here he thought? Someone touched his hand.

'Welcome back Joe. We thought we'd lost you.'

'Is that you Annie? I can't see you.'

'I'm on this side Joe.' Annie kissed his lips and held his head in her hands. 'I shall always be by your side.'

Joe finally regained sufficient consciousness to look around his room. 'Not bad is it? Could do with a lick of paint, but it'll do for me.' He smiled at Annie. 'What happened?'

'We found you, or rather the police found you by the Land Rover. You'd passed out after calling in to give them the directions to where Kate and that murderer were.'

Joe frowned. Then realisation hit him. 'Is she all right? Did they get that murdering bastard? Oh, sorry for the language.'

'I don't blame you. From what they have told me, he deserved everything he got. But he's not dead you know. Kate is fine and safe at last.'

'I'm glad.'

The door opened and in walked Kate and Adam. 'Hi Joe,' Kate said. 'Hope we're not disturbing this little love nest.' Her laughter was a tonic to Joe who whooped with joy as far as he could.

'Steady Joe. You're not back to full health yet. You were nearly a gonner you know.' Kate bent and kissed his forehead. 'Thanks for calling the troops in Joe. Couldn't have managed without you.' She looked at Adam and acknowledged his slight nod that she hadn't revealed his part in the rescue.

Annie pulled his hand closer. 'So what happened Joe? Can you remember?'

'Yes I can,' Joe replied. 'It's as clear as spring water now. But I don't know if I can convince you of what happened. I can hardly believe it myself.'

'Why Joe?'

'Because no one will believe it. Did you see anything Kate?' He turned to her in the vain hope that she had witnessed what had happened.

Kate shook her head. 'Tell us exactly how you managed to get to the shore Joe. I remember Angus shooting you – I thought that he had killed you – and then he shot out the engine. You were marooned in the middle of the loch.'

'I was wasn't I? I couldn't move. The shot hit me in the back and I couldn't move my arms. The engine was useless .....and then ... then ... well the dinghy started to move forward to the other side of the loch. On its own. I was doing nothing. It moved straight ahead as if someone or something was pulling it.'

The three visitors looked at each other and said nothing.

'I was lying over the gunnel on the left hand side. The mooring rope was trailing loose ahead of the dinghy. Suddenly it was taut. And then the boat moved. It was dark but I could just see a dark shape at the end of the rope pulling. Like a round hump or something. It moved up and down like a whale swimming.' Joe looked for some understanding from those present, but saw only blank faces.

'You were in a sort of coma Joe. The doctor said so. It must have been the current that brought you to shore. Or the wind.' Annie didn't sound very convincing and shrugged her shoulders. 'The most important thing is that you are safe and that you can get your strength back so that you are ready for the big day.'

'Big day?' said Kate, her brows knitting into an arch.

'Wedding day. Before all this happened Joe asked me to marry him, and I said yes,' she declared triumphantly.

They all burst into congratulations and shaking of hands and kisses and all Joe's explanations were lost in the reverie.

'Don't forget to ask us to the wedding will you?' laughed Kate. She looked at Adam and signalled that they should leave the lovers to themselves.

'Bye Joe. You did a great job. Annie's lucky to have a man like you.' Adam's salute was answered by Annie.

'And he's lucky to have a woman like me!'

'You know something Adam that you are not telling. What pulled Joe ashore?'

Adam turned to Kate with a smile. 'You wouldn't believe me, isn't that what Joe said?' He uttered a chuckle. 'I'll tell you all, including how I knew Joe had reached the shore and that the police were on their way.'

Kate waited impatiently.

'Later,' said Adam.

Chapter Sixty Three

'You haven't quite recovered from your experience have you Kate?' Adam's question hung in the sharp frosty air like an icicle from a gutter.

'No. I can't figure out exactly what Angus was hoping to gain. He had no chance of getting away this time. His mind seemed to have collapsed completely.'

Adam put his arm around Kate as they walked by the loch. 'Who knows what evils are in men's minds?'

'Is that what you think it is Adam? Evil? Are men born that way or do they gradually unearth bestial traits that have lain dormant for years? He was never like that. He was wild and reckless yes, but to sink to that level is depravity at its worst.' Kate shook her head and clung onto Adam's hand.

'What else troubles you Kate? I see a trace of uncertainty in your eyes now and then. What are you not happy about?' Adam stopped and sat her on one of the benches, hopefully put there for the visitors. Very rarely used.

Kate looked closely at his compassionate expression. 'Adam. When Angus was threatening me with the knife, where were you? That was the most terrifying moment of my life. I needed you so much then. Our baby … I thought it was the end.'

'No my love. I was quite close. I was watching Angus, ready for a shot. I wouldn't have let him harm you.'

'But .. but what was that horse doing there? A horse Adam. Suddenly appearing from nowhere.' She turned suddenly to him. 'And then you shot it.'

'Yes Kate. I destroyed the evil that exists in most forms of life. Not just the usual killing for food, but a lust that is built in to some beings that defies description.' Adam's face contorted into a pained anguish that Kate had not seen before.

'When it stood there quietly looking at Angus, I had an eerie feeling that it was .... it was .. not an animal.'

'What did you think it was Kate?'

Her face incredulous, Kate blurted out. 'I thought it was you!' She stopped and examined Adam's face as the pain in it engulfed him.

'No Kate. It was not me.' He tried to speak but it came out as a whimper. 'He was my brother.'

'You mean .... you mean .. it was a kelpie, or whatever they call them?' Then Kate realised what Adam had just said. 'Your brother!? How? What do you ...?'

'Kate. You have every reason to be confused. If you promise to listen for the next few minutes I will explain everything. But one important point you must keep in mind above all things, is that I love you.'

'That's the first time that you have said that Adam.' Kate returned his embrace. 'But I am so confused that the bond that we have between us is threatened by your past. Tell me Adam. Tell me all of the truth.'

'I will Kate.' Adam took a deep breath. 'Firstly I am not as you think, a kelpie. Or water horse or anything like that. I am a human. Just like you. That is why I can now tell you that I love you beyond anything I have ever felt before. But.' His eyes swept the glass like surface of the loch as if seeking words to put into some sort of meaningful order. 'But what I am about to tell you may destroy the love that I know you have for me.'

Kate trembled, her mind in a whirl. So much had happened in so short a time. She needed to be utterly convinced and any doubts removed once and for all. She waited for Adam to speak.

'I lived for most of my life in a hamlet far north of here with a wonderful couple of farmers who spent their life devoted to me. They nurtured me, fed me, educated me, taught me about life and about the world around. They were simple people, but the salt of the earth. I owe my life to them. They adopted me when I was a baby and instilled in me a sense of pride and goodness that they held so dear. It was almost god-like. So beneficent were they that they abhorred all things that went against the laws of the ten commandments. But I was also taught to have compassion and a sense of justice. Sometimes that is very difficult.'

Kate did not utter a word.

'You may ask why I was adopted. It was because my true parents could not raise me in the manner that they had chosen for me. The world was barred to them, so they conceived a strategy that might give me the future for which they prayed. A new beginning for them and a fulfilment of their dream.

'You see, they had become aware over the years of their life that the development of their family had come to its ultimate evolution. They needed to see that their species would outlive the present form and take its place among the most enhanced life on earth.'

Adam paused. He saw the wonderment in Kate's eyes as she looked deep into his.

'Let me try and explain how my kind view life.' Kate sucked in a breath at the "my kind" quote. He continued. 'In your world the outer appearance is of paramount importance. It is broadcast and advertised in every media type there is. People fall in love with the "image" before they have a chance to seek out the inner beauty. But what of blind persons? They fall in love with the person's nature, their personality. A something that cannot be measured by the outer shell. Ugly people love each other despite their looks. It is a myth that remains a great part of the break up of a lot of marriages. The outer shell is attractive for so long and then the real soul is discovered not to be as beautiful as the façade. Angus for instance,' Adam shook his head. 'Did you ever doubt him in the early days? Did his evil surface before he lost his mind?'

Kate took a breath. 'You say that you were taught right and wrong and the ethics of good conduct. Did those same ethics rule you when you shot that water horse or kelpie?'

'Yes Kate, they did. I was destined to destroy that water horse. That was a judgement my family passed on to me. It too had the evil inside.'

'But when the shots rang out, and it died in that horrible fashion, you filled up and you almost cried. I have never seen you do that before.'

Adam swept the loch with his dark brown eyes shielded by perfect lashes. 'It was the hardest task I have ever been set Kate. You see ….. despite everything, I loved my brother. He was born before me and soon my parents realised that he was not the progeny that would enhance their lives. So they came onto the land and assumed the human form. They lived as humans until my birth. I was conceived while they were human, so my genealogy is undoubted. I can never revert to the kelpie form again.

'But. My brother was a different matter. Whether he was jealous of me or some other misconceived fault, I do not know. He was a renegade. He was responsible for terrible deaths around the lochs and had to be stopped. My parents gave me that task. It could only be done with a special type of bullet. Kelpies in water horse form are not of the same elements as humans and can only by killed by a special mineral. Atomic number 72 – Hafnium. One bullet to the frontal lobe destroying balance co-ordination and posture. The other to the cerebellum to shatter the behaviour and personality complex. That is how he died.'

'Oh Adam. To kill your own brother.' Kate's mind was in a whirl. What had she committed herself to? And her baby?

'If you cannot accept my heritage, then so be it, but hear me out. A long time ago, the human race was just crawling out of the sea in the most bizarre forms ever imaginable. From those, the present life on earth was begun. And it is still developing. Our form of life, by contrast was something that is dear to most people's hearts. Who has not had the love of a horse? The devotion and affection from a pet? The soul or the psyche is the secret. What they are thinking, but are unable to say. What their feelings are and the inability to express them only by gestures. My kind have accelerated that process in one enormous jump. Me. I am human and will remain human, but I still love my parents as they love me.'

Kate took a deep breath. 'Adam, this is like a shock to the system. I can't take it in yet. I love you, I know that. Will that alter because of where you came from? Logically I should reject any sort of love between us, but you have explained the wider picture and it makes sense. I love you and what is in you. Compassion for your brother, despite his evil. Love of you parents whatever they are. And your love for me and the honourable manner that you have demonstrated since I have known you. One question.'

'Yes?'

'Were you in love with me when we first made love, or was that just a duty?'

'Yes, I loved you. But since I had never known love before, I did not recognise it for what it was. The deep relationship between us only rooted itself as I felt that I couldn't live without you. Our baby was a blessing, but not the object of my love for you. I want to be with you; to have more babies; to look after you until the end of my days.'

Kate cried. She sobbed into Adam's arms as he held her close and brushed his lips over her lustrous hair. 'Think of us as a beginning Kate. A noble family if you like. With standards that need re-introducing to the world. A sense of justice and fairness that can be spread by our offspring and gradually, given God's help, it will inoculate the world against the present malady of self and materialism.'

Chapter Sixty Four

'Thank you Kate. I appreciate you ringing me to bring me up to date with everything. You must have suffered another trauma from what you have told me. I couldn't have sustained that experience. But then, I always knew you were the strong type. Well done. We shall miss you terribly, but I fully understand your decision.' Detective Inspector Baddeley rang off with a final wish for Kate's happiness.

Kate was pleased that she had at last decided to hand in her resignation to the police force. Life in Scotland was everything that she had missed in the merry-go-round of Manchester with its never ending calendar of crime and so called self justification as an excuse for living.

She would not miss it. Her baby was the prime motivation for her new life.

The sadness of lost friends occupied her mind more than she would have wished, but she still mourned the death of Annie's ex-husband, Joe's partner in the police, and the three little innocent girls, caught up in a web not of their doing.

Angus would spend the rest of his life in Broadmoor. A wasted life? Or one which had been twisted by fate? She would never know.

Annie was to be married to Joe. A union that had acquired universal applause from all of her friends. Especially Kate. 'Keep him this time Annie,' she had whispered. 'He is the one.'

'Don't worry Kate. I will do everything he says. After all he's the law isn't he?' And they both had collapsed in peels of laughter that came from the heart.

Adam was right, Kate thought. That indiscernible something in us that welds an understanding no matter what physical attributes may exist. I have learnt to view the world with a new vision that gives me a better comprehension of life and the joy of life that is there for the taking.

She folded the baby clothes, touching them tenderly as she thought of when they would adorn the love of her life. Tinted with blue and decorated with a pretty blue ribbon pattern. A boy. Now she had no doubt. Her sense of wonder overwhelmed her as she imagined her future son. There was only the tiniest glimmer of hesitation as she felt her stomach and the gentlest of kicks as he grew within her.

Chapter Sixty Five

We are more than content. The sadness of our loss is offset by the joy in what you have achieved. This is the culmination of the years of hope. Our dream and the dream of future generations is safe in your hands. Although you are not of our kind now, we know that your thoughts are with us and that the love we share can never be threatened.

I am pleased that your wishes have been perfected. And I am honoured that you chose me to be the bearer of your ambition. The life I have now is more than justification for what was intended. So many opportunities; so much promise; the vista of my life is far beyond what could have ever been contemplated. You were the pioneers of a new beginning and can rest content that the virtues held so dear to our kind will be perpetuated in future generations.

We shall watch your progress and that of your son. You are always in our minds..

Chapter Sixty Six

There was that certain nip in the air that sometimes comes with the November weather. A cold, almost chapping wind that ignores the idle wrappings of the unwary and chills the bones.

Trees drip with hoary frost, water shows signs of silvery slates atop the surface and breath is almost solid.

Kate stood gazing at the vista. Still enthralled with the wonder of it all, she moved effortlessly with the pushchair along the shore of Loch Garve. Pretty now somehow. The mystery had gone. The silence had been awakened from its slumber and sang as if a choir was being orchestrated. Birds no longer avoided the waters. Animals came and drank the precious liquid. People no longer avoided the spot. Beautiful and dominating in its glory, it was a portrait matching any of Turner's landscapes.

Kate looked down at her son. A spitting image of Adam. She liked that. Dark and handsome, with smooth cheeks and strong limbs. The eyes held her fascination. Dark pools of reflected love. She adored him. He laughed and jumped his arms up and down as if to say pick me up.

She did so. Solid as a rock, but with the taut muscles giving a welcoming warmth.

Kate cast her gaze along the loch shores until they fastened on a point to the north west. Clear as a bell now with the pines casting their long reflections almost to where she stood. There was a movement which she couldn't quite distinguish. Some mist appearing at a spot over the deepest part of the loch. It continued to rise as if drawn up by its warmth. She smiled. Only a chimney could make a smoke column like that.

Adam's parents had returned to their home. He had promised to teach her how to communicate by mind as he did on that dreadful night so long ago to learn the truth about Joe.

They would continue to fool the public in Loch Ness from time to time, one behind the other creating "the monster" as Adam had jokingly put it.

All was right with the world.

She grasped her little boy more tightly and slid her hand under his bottom. Through the clothing she felt the coccygeal vertebra pressing into her palm. A little longer than normal she had been told by the doctor, but exactly the same as the one she fondled so often when making love to Adam.

She felt complete.